"Do I scare you that much?" Simon asked.

"You don't scare me one bit," Shanna replied, her hands on her hips. "But I'm pretty sure I scare you. We all scare you. You know, you could be a good example to these kids. Come on out and play with us sometime, maybe?"

"I don't know about that." Simon patted the dog at his side.

She nodded, then cooed at the dog, Shiloh, the sound of her gentle words making a funny little shiver do its own two-step down Simon's backbone. "You can send Shiloh over anytime."

The dare was back and he couldn't resist it. "And what about me? Am I invited back for s'mores next time you have a picnic?"

She seemed shocked, her expressive eyes widening. "I thought you'd rather not share in our little picnics out here. Or any other part of our happenings here, for that matter."

She had him there. He'd made it pretty clear he wanted to be [illegible] ave to put out anot [illegible]

She smiled.

Books by Lenora Worth

Love Inspired

†*The Carpenter's Wife*
†*Heart of Stone*
†*A Tender Touch*
Blessed Bouquets
"The Dream Man"
**A Certain Hope*
**A Perfect Love*
**A Leap of Faith*
Christmas Homecoming
Mountain Sanctuary
Lone Star Secret
Gift of Wonder
The Perfect Gift
Hometown Princess
Hometown Sweetheart

†Sunset Island
*Texas Hearts

Love Inspired Suspense

A Face in the Shadows
Heart of the Night
Code of Honor
Risky Reunion
Assignment: Bodyguard
The Soldier's Mission
Body of Evidence

Steeple Hill

After the Storm
Echoes of Danger
Once Upon a Christmas
"'Twas the Week Before Christmas"

LENORA WORTH

has written more than forty books for three different publishers. Her career with Steeple Hill Books spans close to fourteen years. Her very first Love Inspired title, *The Wedding Quilt,* won *Affaire de Coeur*'s Best Inspirational for 1997, and *Logan's Child* won an *RT Book Reviews* Best Love Inspired for 1998. With millions of books in print, Lenora continues to write for the Love Inspired and Love Inspired Suspense lines. Lenora also wrote a weekly opinion column for the local paper and worked freelance for years with a local magazine. She has now turned to full-time fiction writing and enjoying adventures with her retired husband, Don. Married for thirty-five years, they have two grown children. Lenora enjoys writing, reading and shopping…especially shoe shopping.

Hometown Sweetheart

Lenora Worth

Love Inspired

Recycling programs for this product may not exist in your area.

ISBN-13: 978-0-373-81540-1

HOMETOWN SWEETHEART

www.LoveInspiredBooks.com

Printed in U.S.A.

My foot has held fast to His steps;
I have kept His way and not turned aside.
—*Job* 23:11

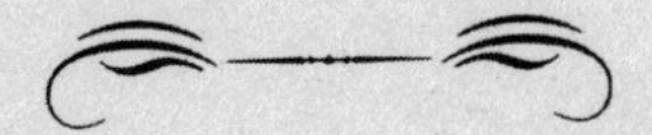

To my nephew Jeremy Smith,
a true cowboy in spirit.

Chapter One

What was that infernal noise?

Simon Adams winced as he lost concentration yet again. Turning from the pair of boots he'd been working on for the last three hours, Simon grunted. That famous country singer in Nashville would just have to wait a while longer to get his handmade boots.

Right now Simon had to go outside and find out what was going on across the fence in what used to be a vacant vacation cabin. A cabin nestled in the riotous spring beauty of the Blue Ridge Mountains of North Georgia near the little river town of Knotwood.

There it went again. The banging and knocking, the giggling and shouting.

People.

Simon didn't like people.

His brother's dog, Shiloh—he really didn't like the dog either—followed Simon out the double doors of his workshop, barking at the unusual noises echoing over the woods and trees. Obviously Shiloh was more excited about this intrusion than Simon. They both enjoyed the quiet of the countryside, but the dog craved company.

"Quit your whining," Simon said to the big golden retriever. "We don't need company today."

Stalking up to the fence line, he couldn't believe his eyes. Someone was moving into the big, sprawling cabin next to his. Okay, maybe a hundred yards from his, but still too close for comfort.

Shiloh barked again, a friendly let's-go-see-who-it-is kind of bark.

"No," Simon told the dog. "Why didn't you go into town with Rick anyway?"

Shiloh appeared sheepish then turned to stare at what looked like an army of people in all kinds of sizes and shapes lining up in front of the house to unload a big passenger van. Small people.

"Great. Kids." Just what he needed. He didn't really like kids, either.

Shifting on his old work boots, Simon ignored the fresh spring air filled with the scent of honeysuckle and the sound of birds chirping in a church choir harmony. He pushed thoughts of his deceased wife Marcy out of his mind. He'd never hear his own children laughing. And he didn't want to hear these particular children—seven of them at last count—next door to his studio day in and day out for who knew how long. They only reminded him of what he would never have.

"This is not good, dog," he said to Shiloh. Not good at all. He liked his seclusion. He liked being alone.

Frustrated, he turned to go back inside when a woman emerged from the cabin and clapped her hands together. "Finish up and we'll start the campfire and cook some hot-dogs. The best you'll ever eat in your life, I promise."

The woman had dark curly hair falling in layers around her porcelain face and a pretty smile that could probably charm those twittering birds. She wore jeans and a bright pink shirt, a plaid scarf notched around her neck at a jaunty angle, making her stand out against the green woods.

Nice.

Shiloh barked his approval and before Simon could hide, the woman glanced over and looked right at him. Then she came prancing over to the fence.

"Hello, neighbor," she said, waving as if he were a long-lost friend, her perky smile broadening, her eyes as blue as the sky. "I'm Shanna. Shanna White."

He really didn't like perky. "Simon," he said with a grunt while she bent down to pet Shiloh through the fence.

"You're Rick's brother," she replied, smiling at Shiloh. "Cari told me all about you." Then she lifted up to stare at him. "She also told me you don't like to be bothered. Sorry if we interrupted your work."

That was certainly direct. Simon stumbled through his words. "It's okay. Nice to meet you."

"Same here," Shanna said. "We'll be here during spring break, doing the usual things—hiking, fishing, rafting on the river, cookouts around the campfire."

"And how long is…uh…spring break?"

Giving him a mock frown, she said, "All next week. We're here from today to next Saturday. I'd better get back to the troops. I have one very young one over there and even though her grandmother came along to chaperone, Katie's a handful—eight years old and wanting to hang with the older kids. I'm sure we'll see you again, though."

Relieved, Simon nodded and turned to hightail it back to his own place. Today was Saturday. One whole week. He didn't want them to be here for spring break. He didn't want to see them again. He didn't want to engage in small talk.

He didn't want to engage at all.

But he couldn't help looking back and listening to the sound of Shanna White's enticing laughter floating over the trees. How was a man supposed to drown that out?

About an hour later he smelled smoke. Since he didn't have a fire going in the massive fireplace centered on one wall in his workshop, Simon decided this smoke might be coming from another fire. A campfire or grill, maybe?

A hint of lighter fluid wafted across his nostrils.

Then he heard shouts. Glancing out the big window, he saw the source of this new interruption. His neighbor was trying to start a campfire behind her cabin. And all of those little hooligans were helping her. More like hindering her, Simon thought on a huff.

He watched while she doused the wood with lighter fluid then touched a match to the wood. He kept on watching when one of the kids kicked at the wet wood and said something no preteen should ever say, when the fire seemed to spurt and then fizzle.

Fascinated in spite of being interrupted, Simon went out onto the porch and listened.

"We ain't never gonna get this fire started, Miss Shanna. And I'm starving."

"Just relax, Felix. We'll figure this out."

"Were you a Girl Scout, Miss Shanna?" one of the younger girls asked.

"I don't think she was," the older teen

Simon recognized as Brady Stillman said, his tone bored and full of tempered anger. Simon had seen the kid around his brother's general store in town. He worked there after school.

"I was in Scouts until my daddy left and my mom had to go back to work," another kid chimed in. "We learned how to make fire by rubbing two sticks together. Want me to show you?"

"No," everyone said together.

The smile forming on Simon's face surprised him even while it irritated him. Good grief, he had work to do.

He turned to get back to that work when a flash of blue-smoked flames caught his eye. Good, they got the fire started.

Then he heard kids hollering and screaming, followed by that lilting little voice shouting, "It's okay, kids. I've got this under control."

Yeah right, Simon thought as he grabbed a rake nestled by the door and headed down the steps. She had it under control all right. Miss Shanna was about to set the woods on fire.

* * *

Shanna watched as the fire shot up toward the oak trees and sweet gums, her heart surging in concern. She could handle this. She'd just…toss leaves and dirt on it. Yes, that would work. The leaves were still wet from the recent storm that has passed through. Thinking that would do the trick, she called out to the group. "Leaves. Grab some leaves to put on the fire."

That brought a scramble of feet and arms all rushing to gather debris, the chaos mounting while the fire blazed higher and wider. Then a rain of wet, decaying leaves fell down around her, most of them missing the center of the fire and making the whole thing worse by bringing out a heavy fog of smoke.

Coughing, Shanna waved her gloved hands. "That's enough. I don't think that's helping."

"What should we do now?" Pamela asked, her long blond hair falling around her face as she bent toward the fire.

"Get back," Shanna said, yanking the girl away before her curls got singed.

"Can we cook the hotdogs now?" Marshall, known for his outbursts and for pulling practical jokes on his friends, asked with a grin. "They'll sure get roasted in that big fire."

"No, not yet," she said. "We want the fire to die down first." She hoped this inferno would settle down.

Katie's grandmother Janie called from the small back deck. "Need any help, Shanna?"

"No, ma'am. Just stay up there," Shanna called back. She couldn't risk Katie's grandmother falling and hurting herself. "We've got things under control."

Brady waved a hand over his nose. "This fire's getting bigger and bigger. I don't think it's gonna die anytime soon. This whole picnic is lame."

Shanna watched as he stomped off toward the cabin. "Brady, come back here."

Brady kept right on walking.

"I'm with him," Felix said, his dark dreadlocks bouncing with attitude as he shuffled toward Brady. "I'll find a pack of crackers."

"I want hotdogs," little Katie said on a

wail. “I want a picnic and some of them s’more things Miss Shanna told us about.”

“It’s all right, Katie,” Shanna said, trying to corral both the growing fire and the disappointed children. “We’ll get the fire down and I’ll start the wienie roast, I promise.”

She looked up as the fire licked at the jagged limb of a dry-rotted oak tree and then with a whish ignited the tree like kindling. This fire was getting out of control and she had no way of putting it out.

Then she saw Katie smiling and pointing and turned just in time to feel the cold wet spray of water hitting above her head. “What—”

Simon Adams stood there with a water hose positioned with a powerful spray toward the tree that had caught on fire. Without a word, he soaked down the blaze.

And he didn’t look too happy.

“There’s your fire,” Simon told Shanna a few minutes later. “Now enjoy your…uh… picnic.”

She at least had the grace to look embarrassed. “I’m sorry,” she said, her tone low.

"You can go back to work now. I'll take it from here."

Surprised at the way she spun around in dismissal, Simon bristled. He wasn't accustomed to being dismissed, especially after he'd dropped everything to help her.

"You're welcome," he called while she handed out long forked sticks with hotdogs stuck on them and went about supervising this wienie-roast gone bad.

"Hold up, Mr. Adams." She turned back toward him then, her usual perkiness subdued into a look of disappointment and dismay. Was she going to cry? 'Cause he didn't like crying women and he sure didn't have time to console someone who'd been foolish to begin with.

But Shanna White wasn't about to cry. No sir. She came stomping toward him with a bit of her own fire shooting through her pretty edge-of-sky blue eyes, stopping with a skid of a halt inches from his nose. "I do so appreciate your help in getting this fire under control, but I don't appreciate the condescending way you oh-so-carefully explained loudly enough to wake the bears about how to start a campfire and keep it from...how did you put that?...burning down the whole mountainside."

She leaned closer still, the scent of her flowery perfume mixed with the smell of lighter fluid-engulfed wood. "I'm trying here, okay? These kids need *good* examples, not some snarky man who has a chip bigger than that old tree on his shoulder. So back off, will you?" Then before he could catch his breath, she added, "Of course, you're welcome to share a hotdog and some s'mores with us, since you did save the day, so to speak."

Dumbfounded, Simon smiled for the second time that day. Then quickly went back to frowning. "I don't want a hotdog, lady. I want some peace and quiet. If you can give me that, then I'll gladly leave you to your own devices. As long as they don't interfere with me or my work."

She glared at him. It was a dainty glare but it meant business. "Well, we wouldn't want that now, would we? We'll try to whisper all week. You know, teenagers and preteens are so very good at that. Don't worry. I think they're all terrified of you anyway.

If you'll excuse me, I have some s'mores to make."

Dismissed yet again, Simon stood there with his hands in his pockets, the amused and way-too-interested gazes coming from seven sets of eyes making him hot under the collar. Or maybe it was the scalding takedown he'd just been given by Miss Shanna that had him hot under the collar. Either way, he refused to stand here and be insulted after he'd taken the time to help her.

Simon glanced over at the kids, noting that some of them were actually enjoying cooking their hotdogs on sticks. Then memories of another picnic not far from here swirled like embers in front of his eyes. He could hear Marcy's sweet laughter, see her sparkling eyes, feel her in his arms as he tried to keep her warm. An acute anger and longing filled his heart, causing him to step back from the scene in front of him.

"I won't bother you again if you promise to leave me alone," he said.

And without a word, he hurried back to the studio where Shiloh whimpered at the door. Simon let the big dog out. The dog could go entertain the neighbors. *He* wanted to be alone. Completely alone. So he shut the door and cranked up the country music he liked to listen to while he worked.

And with a determined effort, he put Shanna White and her seven charges out of his mind. Or at least as far away from his thoughts as he could, considering that for the rest of the long afternoon, he heard her occasional bursts of tingling laughter, even over the twang of the somebody-done-somebody-wrong love songs.

"That young man certainly had a burr in his bonnet," Janie said after Simon was out of earshot. "Or more like, a burr in his cowboy boot."

"He doesn't like being around other people," Shanna said. "It distracts him from his work." And his pain. Shanna knew why he was hiding, and it caused her to be more sympathetic.

"Maybe he needs distracting," Janie said. Then she turned toward the cabin and walked away, smiling.

Shanna watched as her new neighbor hurried inside his big barnlike studio, his faithful dog waiting for him. But he let the dog out then shut the door in the dog's face, too.

No surprise there, she thought with an amused smile. She'd been warned that her neighbor was reclusive and standoffish. Her friend Cari Duncan—now Cari Duncan Adams—had also warned her about Simon's dark good looks and even darker not-so-friendly scowls. Cari was newly married to Simon's younger brother Rick. Rick, along with his mother Gayle, ran Adams' General Store and Apparel in the quaint village of Knotwood Mountain about ten miles to the south.

But his older brother Simon stayed holed up out here on the family compound near the Chattahoochee River, creating handmade one-of-a-kind boots for everyone from celebrities and politicians to construction workers and cowboys. His work was famous but apparently so was his notorious seclusion. He didn't venture out to get clients. They came begging to him. Everyone wanted a pair of Simon Adams boots. But not everyone could afford them. Including Shanna. And apparently, everyone cowered and tiptoed around his dark moods. Not including Shanna. She had seven unruly wards to worry about. She didn't have time to bow down to His Highness or his demands.

The man made beautiful boots, no doubt about that.

Too bad his attitude toward the entire human race wasn't so beautiful. Cari had explained why Simon was this way. And Shanna sure wasn't going to ask him to get over it. He'd been through the worst.

Telling herself to cut him some slack and pray for him instead of belittling him, Shanna thought about what Cari had told her when she and Rick had insisted Shanna could use this cabin, rent-free, for a week over the spring break.

"I have to explain about Simon," Cari said one night after a church meeting. "He lost his wife Marcy to cancer a few years ago and well, since then he's become a bit of a recluse. He's an artist, so he's naturally temperamental and hard to live with. But Rick told me when we first started dating that his brother hasn't gotten over his wife's death. He's bitter, Shanna. So he might be nasty to you if you approach him. He won't like having neighbors for a week but even the mighty Simon Adams can't dictate who his brother rents that cabin to."

Shanna thought about Cari's words now as she glanced over toward Simon's workshop. No, Simon couldn't keep people away from his brother's property but he could make trouble for her. Especially if this rat pack of wayward teens and younger children bothered him.

She'd talk to her seven charges and explain the rules:

Leave the big man next door alone.

Stay off his property.

Don't get too loud.

Don't mess with the dog.

And no matter what, don't go inside that studio.

Just pretend he's not there.

After seeing the man firsthand, she'd have to remind herself of all those rules, too.

A loud crash inside the cabin caused Shanna to turn and rush inside. This was not going to be an easy week.

Chapter Two

Shanna was up the next morning with the first rays of sunshine. She loved early morning. It was the best time to talk to God while she had a clear head and some quiet time. Being a high school teacher meant she didn't have any spare time during her hectic, structured days. And this week, she wouldn't have much time to herself at all since she was going to be busy each day with a new task for her seven charges.

But right now, she only wanted to voice her prayers to Christ. So she sat in the big comfy chair by the wall of windows in the open den, the fire she'd started earlier crackling, her coffee cup in her hand and her morning notes on her lap. She jotted a few gratitude statements first—*Thank You,*

Lord, for providing us this cabin. Thank You for Rick and Cari and please continue to bless them in their new marriage. Thank You for these children You've brought me to and help me to show them the way to Your love.

Holding her pen in midair, Shanna looked out across the way toward the big looming brown barn with the mural of a pair of cowboy boots on its side. Those giant boots with the famous golden soles were the only sign that Simon Adams actually was a real live human being.

Smiling, Shanna jotted one more thing in her journal. *And thank You, Lord, for Simon Adams. He brings people joy with his art and his creations, even if he does have a bad attitude right now. Help him to heal, Lord.*

Shanna shut the journal with a clap then closed her eyes for a prayer to get her through the day. She'd call Aunt Claire and give her an update and chat a while before the kids woke up. Then they'd start out with a long hike so she could show the kids that God's world was beautiful in spite of the struggles in their lives. She'd also planned a picnic out by the river—just sandwiches and chips—no fires involved. She planned to sing praise songs and give a short devotional followed by some heart-to-heart discussion.

She wanted these kids to have a happy camping experience. Most of them had problems with either school or their life at home and parents who were too busy and frazzled to take them camping. Amazing to think that some parents were either too busy or self-absorbed and bitter to give their children the simple pleasures in life. Or worse, some took out their frustrations on their children. Katie's stepfather had done that, using the child as a punching bag. Katie was safe now, living with her grandparents. And even though she was young, she'd so wanted to come on this trip.

Shanna remembered her own upbringing. She knew firsthand how a child could suffer because of neglect and abuse, didn't she? But she'd overcome all that. She wanted to show these children they could do the same. Especially Katie.

No wonder these kids were confused and troubled. But Shanna couldn't judge them or their parents. She'd seen and heard all kinds of excuses in her five years of teaching in Savannah. Why would things be any different here in Knotwood Mountain?

When she heard a door slamming, she opened her eyes to see Simon Adams emerging from his cabin, a cup of coffee in his hand and that adorable dog trotting at his side. Using this opportunity to spy on him, Shanna stood up to take her own sweet time looking at Simon. He wore jeans, battered boots and a lightweight denim jacket he'd probably bought at his brother's store. His dark hair was shaggy and wild, as if he'd gotten out of bed and dressed in a hurry without even combing it. But then, there was something primitive and wild about the man anyway from what Shanna could see. He didn't walk or stroll, he stalked. He didn't smile or talk to the dog. He scowled with an intensity that bordered on anger. Maybe he *was* angry but even an angry man had to take a breath to remind himself he was alive, didn't he?

Then, as if he knew she were watching, Simon turned and looked right at her, a solid frown marring his otherwise handsome face. Shanna waved a timid wave and watched as he turned and opened the big doors to the studio and quickly disappeared inside, shutting himself away from the world.

And shutting everyone in that world out of his life.

Simon stretched, the muscles in his neck and back protesting while his stomach growled for nourishment. He'd forgotten to eat again. And now sundown was fast approaching.

But the boots were done.

Rich brown leather with swirling tan inlays that reminded Simon of angel wings. The singer had been specific about what he wanted on his boots. And Simon had been determined to oblige the man. Especially since he was paying good money for these one-of-a-kind boots.

Simon was methodical and meticulous about his craft. Making a pair of custom boots could take weeks or months, depending on the entire process and the customer's request.

But at the end of the day, Simon could

always know he'd given it his best. And that's why he had orders well into the next couple of years. He was blessed to do something he loved. Blessed to have busy work.

He was blessed to have something to do to keep his mind off the ever-present loneliness that always set in at dusk—that time of day when loved ones came home from work and families gathered together to share their day and eat.

Looking at the clock, he figured his mother was probably getting ready for bed right now, nestled in her own cabin around the bend from the larger one Simon had shared for years with his brother Rick. It had been the family home when his father was alive but his mother had insisted on moving into the smaller one a few years ago. She'd done that so Simon and Marcy could have some privacy.

After Marcy's death, Rick had somehow managed to move back in part-time and he'd brought that aggravating mutt Shiloh with him. They made annoying roommates.

Simon didn't want or need the company.

Or so he thought. Now he was alone in the big cabin next to his studio.

Rick had gone and gotten himself married to cute little Cari Duncan. What a match that had turned out to be. Now they lived in town for the most part, in the big Victorian house Cari had renovated, conveniently located right next door to the general store. Cari ran her own "girlie" boutique on the bottom floor of the house and they lived in the spacious upstairs apartment and sometimes came out to the Adams compound on the weekends.

Yeah, a match made in Heaven.

He'd had that once, Simon thought now as he rummaged through the pantry for a can of soup.

Once.

But not anymore. Never again for him.

He couldn't help but wonder what his neighbors were doing tonight. He'd managed to steer clear of Shanna and the Seven NoiseMakers for most of their second day here, thankfully. Not that he was counting.

Now, he'd almost welcome some noise,

some shouts, some sort of accident waiting to happen.

Turning to Shiloh, he said, “I guess it’s just you and me, dog. Maybe my lovesick brother will remember you’re actually his and come and fetch you soon.”

Shiloh barked a gruff rebuttal.

But both Simon and the dog knew they only had each other tonight. And probably for many nights to come. It would have to do. And Simon was pretty sure Rick left Shiloh here on purpose for that very reason, even though his brother used the excuse of big dogs being like bulls in a china shop when it came to the general store.

Simon heated up the can of beefy soup his mother had brought in with her weekly supply of groceries earlier in the week and sat down to watch an old western on the cable channel.

The phone rang right on time. “Goof grief, Mama, why can’t you ever just let a man be?” He said this out loud before he actually answered the phone. “Hello, Ma.”

“Did you eat?”

“I’m eating right now.”

"It's a little late for supper, Simon."

"I worked late."

"You always work late."

"I have orders."

She skipped a beat then asked, "So, what do you think about your new neighbors?"

Simon frowned then did a shoulder roll. Taking a deep breath, he thanked God for his mother even when he wished she wasn't so nosy. "I can tell you, there's about seven too many of them over there."

"Now Simon, be nice. Shanna is a good friend of Cari's. She's a teacher and she moved here from Savannah last fall to take a job at Knotwood High. She's very good at counseling troubled teens—"

"What?" Simon dropped his spoon. "You mean to tell me my brother rented that place to a bunch of hoodlums?"

"I didn't say that," Gayle replied. "First of all, your brother is letting them stay there free for a week. And second, they aren't exactly hoodlums. They're just kids from church who've been through some rough stuff—some of it just minor trouble at school. She signed up to work with our youth and after hearing some of their stories, Shanna volunteered to take them on a retreat during the school break. I plan on coming out during the week to help her with meals and crowd control."

His appetite gone, Simon groaned. "Well, that's mighty nice of her—and you, Ma—but couldn't she take them to Gatlinburg or Stone Mountain, anywhere besides right next door to me?"

"You don't own the entire mountain, son."

"No, but I do have work to do. How am I supposed to get through my summer orders with all that noise going on? And I'm telling you right now if one of them breaks in here—"

"Simon, have a little faith. These children need guidance and attention. They didn't break out of prison. They just took a few wrong turns or had a bit of trouble in school. Katie McPherson is the youngest and probably the most sensitive. Her grandparents have custody of her now. Be nice to that little girl. And Brady Stillman is one of the older ones. You might remember he did some vandalism to Cari's place when she first moved back last summer."

"Exactly," Simon replied, glaring at Shiloh. "I can't have kids like that snooping around the place." Except maybe that cute little redheaded Katie. She wasn't so bad. She giggled a lot.

"They won't bother you," Gayle said in a mother-tone. "Shanna will make sure they stay on their side of the fence."

"Well, she'd better. I don't like this one bit and I don't like Rick doing this without warning me."

"It's his property to do with as he sees fit," Gayle retorted. "You should be glad he bought it before it went into foreclosure. We need those tourist dollars around here."

"No dollars, Ma, if he's renting the thing for free."

"That's for a good cause."

"I didn't want him buying the property in the first place."

"You wanted it to stay deserted and rundown then?"

"Well, yeah. I liked it way better that way."

"You really are hopeless, you know that?"

"Yes, I am," Simon replied, his blood pressure buzzing. "You'd think my own family would realize that by now."

"We aren't going to give up on you, son," Gayle said, her tone gentle now. "We love you and we'd like you to become a part of the human race again."

"I'm fine with things the way they are."

"Sure you are. Why, anybody could see that."

"I'm going to finish my cold soup now."

"I love you."

Simon let out a sigh. "I love you, too."

He put down the phone and stared into the fire.

He did love his family. But he didn't have anymore love to give to anyone else. He didn't like people around and barely tolerated his brother and his mother. But then, they both knew to leave Simon to his own devices. And they *were* family. Family understood about things. Strangers didn't.

But in spite of Simon's aversion to strangers, he couldn't help but be drawn to the woman in charge of the kids gathered at the cabin next door. And he couldn't help the sweetly hidden thoughts that emerged in his mind like a ray of spring sunshine melting winter snow. Thoughts of a woman and children laughing as they frolicked in the blossoming woods.

Simon got up to stare out the kitchen window.

And then he heard voices lifting out in song.

Shanna had them singing.

Simon listened to the gentle music of a guitar, listened to the old familiar campfire songs he'd learned from his own days at church. The songs were soothing, the voices echoing out over the woods in a time-honored melody.

It was peaceful and pretty, but Simon didn't know how to deal with a woman and seven annoying young people. So he'd do what he'd been doing.

He'd just ignore them. That seemed to work in his dealings with everyone else. And since he'd buried Marcy a few miles away in the old church cemetery, it seemed to be the best solution for him. He wasn't ready to rejoin the human race.

Even on a mild spring night when he was forced to eat cold canned soup and stare at a dog that didn't belong to him, while he secretly eavesdropped on his singing neighbors.

Chapter Three

Shanna petted the golden retriever then offered him the last bite of her hotdog. "I'm not supposed to feed you scraps, I don't think. So let's keep this between the two of us, okay?"

The big dog woofed a reply then looked back up at her with expectant brown eyes.

"No more," Shanna said, her hand on his shaggy back. "I'm in enough trouble with your keeper as it is."

At least today, the group had eaten their hotdogs and chips and they'd even managed to cook their s'mores without anymore mishaps. If she didn't count the boys picking on the girls, Katie falling down and scraping her hand and knee and Brady turning surly at the drop of a hat.

Glancing over at the lanky teen now, Shanna wondered if this week would help the kid. He was on probation for the vandalism since Cari had dropped the charges and suggested community service instead. The judge apparently had agreed to that and according to Cari and Rick, had given the kid a stiff warning. Rick had agreed to give Brady a part-time job after school as part of his sentence, too.

Shanna had met the boy's formidable mother Doreen and his self-centered sister Bridget, so she could certainly understand why he was a troubled child.

When Brady got up and came to sit by her, she took that as a good sign. "What's up, Brady?"

He grabbed at the dog. "Hey, Shiloh."

"Is that his name?" Shanna asked, hoping to strike up a conversation while the other kids played kick ball around the camp. A nice breeze kept the day from being too hot.

Day Three was right on schedule, even if the kids had requested hotdogs again for lunch. They'd had a great morning devotional and discussion, after eating Miss

Janie's amazing pancakes. Then after a long walk, the kids had begged for another campfire meal. At least this time, Shanna hadn't set the woods on fire. Nor had she seen their elusive neighbor either. He was keeping his distance while his dog was enjoying new friends.

Brady kept his eyes on the dog. "Yep. He's Rick's dog but he gets in trouble in town and they don't like to keep him cooped up in the house so he has to stay out here."

With Mr. Personality.

Shanna grinned down at Shiloh. "I'd think a big old dog would love being out here in the country better anyway."

"I sure like it," Brady said, rubbing Shiloh's throat.

"Do you?" Shanna's heart surged with hope. "Are you enjoying things so far?"

He looked at the other kids, his gaze staying on Pamela for a while. "Yeah, I guess. I don't get why I have to hang with all these losers, though."

"Hey, I brought you to help out, remember? You're the oldest one here and I need someone to keep an eye on the younger ones."

"But they're not old enough to be in the youth group at church."

"No, but they'll soon be eligible," she explained. "I want them to be ready to handle that when the time comes."

"Oh, I get it. You're exposing them to a few of us—the few considered the black sheep, first?"

"No, it's not like that," Shanna said, wishing she could find the right words. "I just think it's a good idea for kids of all ages to learn to get along. Unfortunately, each of you here has had issues of some sort at school and with your parents. We have a very diverse group at church so it's important that everyone respects each other at an early age."

"My mom says some of these kids don't belong at our church," he retorted. "She thinks they're beneath us."

Shanna couldn't say what popped into her mind at that comment. But it sure went to show how a parent could influence a child. Did his mother see that her judgments and criticisms rubbed off on her son?

Shanna had seen this firsthand. Her own parents had never attended church and scoffed at Christianity. Thank goodness her aunt had started taking her to church when Shanna was in kindergarten. And thank goodness her Aunt Claire was still her mentor and closest ally in Savannah.

Turning back to Brady, she said, "No one is beneath God's love, Brady. We all fall short but He loves us anyway."

Brady looked serious then nodded. "I guess you're right. I've done some bad stuff but Cari forgave me and invited me to church with her and Rick. She treats me better than my mom and sister, that's for sure."

"Cari is a special person," Shanna replied. "And she loves you a lot."

"But she and my mom still don't get along."

"Well, sometimes being a Christian means you have to let go and just get on with life, even if you can't be best friends with certain people. I'm sure for your sake they're both trying to reconcile."

"At least they don't get into fights any-more like they did when we were growing up."

"That's good and you're the reason for

that truce, I think. They both want what's best for you."

"Yeah, whatever." He got up, bored again. "What's next on our big adventure?"

"Well, speaking of Cari, she and Mrs. Adams are coming out tonight to make spaghetti and then we're going to sing songs around the campfire again. We had fun last night doing that."

"Wow, what a party."

Looked like surly Brady had stepped back in. "I think you'll have a good time. Miss Gayle loves working with the youth."

Brady rolled his eyes. "I guess I can handle it, since I'm kinda stuck out here."

He wandered off to sit with Pamela on a nearby bench, Shiloh following him. The other kids all loved the big dog, too. Checking to make sure everyone was content, Shanna got up to finish clearing their napkins and paper plates. The week had only just started and she was already exhausted. But she had high hopes for this week in the woods. They'd had a good lunch. The kids were comfortable with her and each other now. Some of the teens asked questions that showed they'd listened to her earlier devotional. She wanted these children to know God's unconditional love and she hoped she could show them that she cared about them, too.

"Okay, people. Let's get this cleared up and we'll go for our next hike. There's a pretty spot halfway up the mountain where you can see the whole town of Knotwood. Then we'll come back and go inside to watch one of the movies we rented. After that, dinner and singing."

Shiloh came running toward her but when the big dog almost knocked her down and kept going past her, Shanna turned to see what had caught his attention.

Simon stood at the open gate between their fences, his expression not quite a frown, but not anywhere near a smile, either. But he looked good in his old jeans and even older button-up shirt. He always looked good, even when he seemed so mad.

And just because she loved a challenge, Shanna tossed the rest of her trash in the nearby can and walked over to aggravate him a little bit.

* * *

"Come to fetch your dog?"

Simon saw the hint of dare in her pretty eyes. "He's not my dog."

"Is that why you let him roam around with us every afternoon?"

Not exactly sure why he'd let Shiloh stay out so long, he shifted his feet and glanced over at where the kids were playing ball.

"I forgot he was out," he said, thinking it was the truth. He often let the dog roam around the gated yard but he had forgotten that he'd left the gate between the two properties open when he'd come over to put out the fire the other day. Or maybe he'd left it open on purpose so he'd have an excuse to come over.

She looked from him to his boot shop. "I guess it would be easy to get so caught up in your work you'd forget everything. Even all of us right next door."

He hadn't forgotten her, oh, no. He'd heard her laughing and calling out to the kids. He'd even heard her reading from the Bible and giving a lesson to go along with the Scriptures. But he wouldn't tell her that. "I sure tried."

"Were we too loud and noisy?"

"No. I just turned my music up."

"Oh, right. I thought I heard a Toby Keith song playing earlier."

He shot her his own daring look. "Got something against country music?"

"Not at all. I can dance the two-step with the best of them."

That surprised him. "Really now?"

"Really. My uncle Doug grew up in East Texas and I still visit relatives there all the time."

He let that slide. "I've got customers all over Texas."

"I know. When I told my aunt and uncle I was moving here to take a teaching job, my uncle got all excited. He knows all about Simon Adams boots. He sure admires your work even if he can't afford your cowboy boots."

"I try to adjust my prices for customers," Simon said, his tone defensive even if he'd worked to sound neutral. "I build a basic boot that's fairly reasonable."

"I'll keep that in mind. I do need to get him something for Father's Day."

Father's Day for an uncle? Interesting.

"Too late for this year. I'll be doing good if I get to the orders I'm working on for Christmas."

"It's amazing, what you do," she said, the sincerity in her eyes making Simon think they'd somehow gone past sparring with each other to actually having a conversation. "Your brother brags on your work all the time."

"He just likes the customers my boots bring into the general store."

She grinned at that. "Well, it's nice to be able to get sized for a custom-made pair of boots, I guess."

"I do off-the-shelf boots, too. You know, for the general public. Less expensive."

"Really? Maybe I will be able to afford a pair for my uncle after all. He'd love that."

Simon would make sure her uncle got his boots, if he had to sneak around and get the man's measurements himself. He didn't know why that mattered, but he could be nice when the mood struck him. And looking into her eyes somehow did make him want to be nice.

"What's wrong?" she asked, her tone full of distrust.

"Man, do I scare you that much?"

"You don't scare me one bit," she replied, her hands on her hips. "But I'm pretty sure I scare you. We all scare you. You know, you could be a good example to these kids. Come on out and play with us sometime, maybe? Tell us about your craft, measure some feet for boots—just for fun."

"I don't know about that." Simon patted Shiloh, the steam gone out of his need to pick at her. But the image of her dainty little feet being measured for boots brought logic back into his brain. "I guess I'd better head back and close down the shop."

She nodded then cooed at Shiloh, the sound of her gentle words making a funny little shiver do its own two-step down Simon's backbone.

"You can send Shiloh over anytime."

The dare was back and he couldn't resist it. "And what about me? Am I invited back for s'mores next time you have a picnic?"

She seemed shocked, her expressive eyes widening. "I thought you'd rather not share in our little picnics out here. Or any other part of our happenings here for that matter."

She had him there. He'd made it pretty clear he wanted to be left alone. "I'd rather not have to put out another fire but I like hotdogs."

"Maybe next time then." She turned to spin away then whirled back around. "Hey, your mom is coming later to cook spaghetti. You're welcome to join us."

His mother made the best spaghetti. Thick, rich sauce with fat meatballs. Garlic bread. He couldn't remember the last time he'd had her spaghetti.

"I'd better not—"

They both turned at the sound of a vehicle moving up the winding drive.

His mother. And she had Rick and Cari in the truck with her. Great. Just great. Too late to make a hasty getaway.

"Looks like that's them now. They're early," Shanna said, waving in glee. "Your mother wanted to get a head start, I guess." Shiloh took off, barking his delight.

While Simon stood there, busted and

embarrassed. Because he knew his overly-zealous mother would jump to the wrong conclusion.

But Simon didn't have to worry too much about his mother's assumptions regarding him being caught here talking, no, actually flirting, with a pretty woman.

Oh, no. He knew he was in for some serious ribbing when his brother emerged from the big truck with a grin splitting his face.

"I see you've met Shanna," Rick said, slapping Simon on his back so hard Simon nearly pitched forward.

Wanting to throttle Rick the way he'd done—well, tried to do—all during their growing-up days, Simon took a breath and counted to ten, thankful Shanna was now laughing and talking to Cari and his mother. "I came over to retrieve *your* dog."

Rick let out a snort. "Didn't look like you were in any kind of hurry to take Shiloh home to me."

"I'm leaving—right now."

"Yeah, right." Rick gave him a long hard look. "I do believe I see a sparkle in my old brother's eyes. Coming to talk to the pretty lady—there's a new concept."

Simon wished he'd stayed inside. "I had to be polite, now, didn't I?"

"I didn't think you knew how to be polite."

Gayle walked up, her smile sure and steady. "I saw you talking to Shanna. Isn't she the nicest girl?"

Nice. But certainly not a girl. A woman. Simon had flirted with a woman for the first time since Marcy's death. And that thought alone was enough to sober him into being his old anti-social self.

"Real nice. So nice she just about burned down the woods and the cabin the other afternoon."

With that, he turned and stomped back toward his workshop, leaving his mother and his brother staring a hole through his back.

But when he turned at the door, the only person he saw in the late afternoon sunshine was Shanna White.

And he also saw the hurt, confused look

in her eyes, too. But he told himself it didn't bother him.

Not one bit.

Chapter Four

Three hours later, Simon heard a knock at his door.

He looked out the window but ignored the knock. His brother knocked again.

"What?" he said, opening the door to glare at Rick.

"Get that scowl off your face and come on over for dinner," Rick replied, dragging Simon out by the arm.

"I'm not hungry."

"It's Mom's spaghetti. So I don't believe you. In fact, I bet you've been standing there, sniffing in the wind for the scent of rich Georgia tomatoes and a little basil and olive oil. Am I right?"

Simon couldn't deny it. With all the windows thrown open to the fresh air, he'd taken a sniff or two of the good smells coming from the cabin across the way. His mother let it simmer for hours, making it rich and sweet and good. She knew it was one of his favorite meals.

"Okay, so maybe. I figured Ma would bring me some later anyway."

"Ma, as you insist on calling her, made me come over here to get you. She said and I quote, 'There is certainly no reason Simon can't eat now with the rest of us.'"

Simon could think of a lot of reasons to skip this meal. But he'd never live it down if he did. "Okay, all right. I'll come and eat. But don't expect me to be pleasant."

"I'd never expect that," Rick replied as he headed back down the steps. "But I do expect you to use your manners and treat Shanna with respect."

"I do respect her," Simon shot back. "I've always been a respecter of women."

Rick turned and grinned then. "So you like her just a little bit then?"

Simon would learn one day that he couldn't fool his little brother. "She's a pretty woman. What's not to like?"

"And she's single and available, even if you are about ten years too old for her."

"I'm not that much older than you," Simon said while they walked across the grass. "And besides, I'm not interested. Nice woman, yes. Me, interested, no."

"Whatever you say, brother."

Obviously Rick didn't believe him. Simon wouldn't dare tell his brother that he got these funny little feelings each time Shanna was around. Feelings he didn't want to discuss or even think about. But they were there, like fireflies lighting up the night, inside his head.

Just nerves. He wasn't accustomed to being around a lot of people at once. And he hadn't thought about another woman since Marcy. He didn't like thinking that way.

"Have you met all the kids?" Rick asked, taking the steps to the cabin two at a time.

"No. I've tried to avoid all the kids."

"You're some welcome wagon, that's for sure."

"I only ask to be left alone."

"You need to get out more, get involved in

life." Rick waved his hands. "Look around you, Simon. The dogwoods and magnolias are blooming. The azaleas are budding. The woods are alive with mountain laurel and rhododendrons. It's spring, time for renewal and rebirth."

Simon glanced around the woods. He hated to admit he hadn't even noticed. "I have allergies."

"You do not."

"Do so. I'm allergic to nosy brothers and noisy kids."

Rick stopped at the screen door to the cabin. "No, you're just afraid to live, Simon. And if you don't drop that attitude, one day you'll look up and see that you've missed out on a lot of things."

Simon sniffed, lifting his nose toward the kitchen. "Well, I ain't missing out on that spaghetti. So move out of my way."

"You came."

Shanna smiled over at Simon as she handed him a sturdy foam plate of spaghetti and crusty French bread. "We have pound cake and ice cream for dessert."

"My mom's cake?"

"I do believe so. She's such a good cook."

"Yeah." He took the plate then sat down at one of the long picnic tables he'd helped Rick and some of the boys carry down between the cabins to a level spot closer to the river. "She is a good cook. She taught my wife how to cook."

Shanna looked up at that statement, her eyes filling with compassion. "I'm so sorry about what happened."

Simon wanted to bite his tongue. He never talked to anyone about Marcy. How had that slipped out? "Thanks." He went about shoveling in food, chewing so he wouldn't have to speak.

"You don't like talking about it, do you?"

"No." And he didn't like that she could see that.

"Then we won't."

Shanna sipped her iced tea and stared out into the woods. "It's so peaceful out here."

"Yeah." Or at least it had been until this week.

"Don't you get lonely, though?"

"No."

She sat her cup down. “You’re not making this easy.”

“I’m just being me.”

“Like I said, you’re not making this easy.”

“What do you expect from me?” he said, looking up and into her eyes.

She didn’t back down, even if she did appear hurt. “I heard you telling Rick about how I almost set the woods on fire. If I didn’t have complete confidence in my ability to win people over, I’d certainly have a complex regarding you.”

“Don’t worry about me. I’m just an ornery old bootmaker.”

“You’re not that old, but you are ornery.”

He actually chuckled at that, only because he and Rick had just discussed that very thing.

“Wow, he laughs.”

Simon’s smile stilled on his face. “And she smiles. You’re pretty when you smile.”

She lowered her head then slanted her eyes up at him. “And you don’t look half bad when you laugh.”

“I’m not used to people being around.”

“I know. Your mom told me you didn’t even want Rick to buy the other cabin because you didn't want tourists hanging out back here."

"True. I do have to work for a living."

"But has anyone really ever bothered you?"

"Yeah, you."

"Me?" She shook her head. "I've tried to avoid you. And I've cautioned the kids to do the same. Even though they're fascinated with what you do. Especially little Katie. She thinks you're some sort of Paul Bunyan, a giant of a man."

"Are they that curious about me?" He reckoned he could give the little varmints a tour, just to shut them up. Or say "Boo" to them so they'd leave him alone.

"Yeah. You're like the troll under the bridge to them, part fascinating and part frightening."

"I'm a troll?"

"I said you're like a troll. But you don't look like one, no."

"I do like to hide and jump out at pretty women."

She laughed at that. "Your brother didn't tell me you actually have a sense of humor."

He savored another bite of spaghetti,

the rich sauce tasting spicy and sweet as it went down. "And what *did* my brother tell you?"

She turned serious then. "That you were hurting and you needed time to heal."

Simon dropped his plastic fork, the rich food suddenly stuck in his throat. "You're kind of blunt, aren't you?"

"I believe in the truth. So let's get things out in the open. I had a bad childhood, so I know all about neglect and dysfunction. Some of these children have been through much worse, however. You lost your wife to a horrible disease. You have every reason to be angry at the world. I lost both my parents when I was a child. My father left when I was a baby, so I don't know where he is now. My mother remarried, but…it wasn't a good marriage." She stopped, her vivid eyes going dark. "She died when I was thirteen and…my stepfather died in a wreck shortly after her death. I've seen the worst that grief and pain can bring, so I try to reach out and embrace the world. And I believe in hope. So I hope one day you'll find a way to be happy again."

Neglect. Dysfunction? How could someone so vibrant and bubbly even speak in such terms? "I'm sorry about your childhood," he said, feeling like a jerk. "What happened?"

"Nothing I'm ready to talk about," she said, all the joy erased from her eyes. "Nothing you'd want to hear."

Ready to get back to his solitude so he could remove his foot from his mouth, Simon got up. "Thanks for dinner. I've got to go."

She stomped after him. "I was trying to be honest. I didn't mean to upset you."

"You didn't."

"I told you I wouldn't talk about it and I did. I shouldn't have forced you to talk, since I sure don't like to talk about my past."

"Yep."

"I'm sorry."

Simon whirled toward her as a golden dusk settled around them and the sound of the kids laughing and talking to Rick and Cari echoed up the hill. He caught a whiff of wisteria, the scent reminding him of other spring nights near the river. "I'm sorry, too. Sorry that I'm bitter and ornery and nasty to little kids. But I didn't ask for any of this. I'm not sure I'm ready for any of this, do you understand?"

"I think I do," she said, backing away. "But that's a shame. No one should have to suffer grief all alone, Simon."

"It's the only way I know how," he retorted, his blood boiling with a shimmering rage and a heavy regret.

"Maybe you need to look for a new way, a better way, so you can go on living. That's what I had to do."

"And maybe you should stick to counseling your kids, not a man who only asks for some peace and solitude."

He stared at her long and hard, then turned and walked away. He didn't want to look for a new way. He only wanted to remember what he'd had and lost.

And that was something no one could ever change.

Shanna walked back down to the river, her mind still on Simon. Why had she said those things to him? Why had she gone after him? She didn't even know the man.

But she knew what it felt like to be alone

and hurting. She'd held that same anger at a young age, much like some of these kids were doing. She'd cried herself to sleep at night when her fighting, volatile parents had screamed their rage at each other. Because of their neglect and their obsession with destroying each other, she'd learned the hard way that people didn't have to die to cause grief in your life.

Lord, how can I help these children, or this man?

Had God brought her to these beautiful woods to help Simon?

Or should she do as he'd suggested, mind her own business and get back to counseling the children in her care?

Janie met her on the path. "Have you seen Katie?"

"No, ma'am. I thought she was with you."

Janie shook her head. "She was right there but she had to go to the bathroom. She ran ahead and didn't wait for me to come up here with her."

"I'll go check the cabin," Shanna said. "Why don't you wait down by the tables? It's getting dark."

Then they heard a child's scream echoing down the hill. Followed by a male voice.

"Shanna?"

That was Simon, calling to her. He sounded frantic.

"Shanna, can you come here?"

Shanna ran up the hill. "Wait here, Miss Janie."

"Shanna!"

"Simon?" She searched the long back porch of his cabin then looked inside the brightly lit kitchen and den.

"In here."

Running through the open door, she found Simon sitting on the sofa, holding Katie. The girl was crying her heart out against Simon's shirt.

"I found her when I got inside," he said, rocking the little girl, his hand stroking her hair. He looked as helpless as Katie. "She's bleeding. Her leg."

"Katie, baby, what's wrong?" Shanna said as she dropped to her knees on the braided rug in front of the couch. "What's the matter?"

"I miss my mama," Katie said, gulping back sobs. "I got scared. I came up the hill to go to the bathroom and I came inside the wrong cabin. I got confused and…I tripped on the rug." She burst into tears again.

"Oh, honey, that's all right. I'm sure Simon didn't mind you using his bathroom."

"I didn't," Simon said, glancing at Shanna. "But when she came out and saw me standing in the kitchen, she screamed. I told her it was all right. But she tried to run and she tripped. I sat her down and told her I'd get you. Then I tried to calm her down."

Shanna took Katie into her arms. "Did you think Simon would harm you?"

Katie nodded. "Everyone says he's a mean old man."

Shanna's gaze locked with Simon's. The hurt inside his eyes tore through her. In spite of his moodiness, she didn't believe this man would ever hurt anyone, let alone a frightened little girl. And yet, that's the perception the world had of him.

Lifting Katie up, Shanna held the girl's head in her hands. "Listen to me, Katie. Simon Adams is a very nice man. He's just been out here alone for so long, he's forgotten how to act around other people. It doesn't mean he's a bad person, okay?"

Katie's big eyes searched Simon's face. "I thought he was gonna be mad at me. I didn't want to get a whipping."

"A whipping?" Simon let out a breath. "I'm not mad, Katie. You scared me as much as I scared you. I don't mind you coming inside my house, not at all."

Katie looked doubtful. "Brady said you'd turn into a bear if I bothered you."

Shanna shook her head. "Brady was just teasing you, honey."

"But Marshall told me Simon would grow fangs and look like a wolf."

Simon stood up, his hands moving through his hair, shock clouding his face. Then he turned to face Shanna again. "I'd never—I don't know—"

"It's all right," Shanna said, lifting Katie up onto a stool so she could check Katie's bleeding knee. The girl had reopened the wound from her first fall the other day. "I'll have a talk with those boys. They shouldn't be scaring you that way."

But the damage had been done. And not just to Katie. She'd get over her scare. After all, Simon had tried to comfort her. But he might not forget this night or the harsh accusations the boys had placed on him, all in the name of fun and jokes. He did seem scary, after all. But he also seemed as confused and lost as some of these children.

"I'm sorry," Shanna said, taking Katie up in her arms. "I need to get her back to the cabin so I can check her knee. This is the second time this week she's skinned it in the same place."

Simon nodded, his eyes vacant and faraway. "I scare little children."

Shanna sat Katie down again then hurriedly wet a paper towel and placed it on her leg. "Honey, stay right here, okay, and hold this on your knee. I need to talk to Simon for just a minute. You're okay, right?"

Katie looked up at Simon, bobbing her head, her tears receding. "He wasn't so scary after all, Miss Shanna."

"I know, darling. I saw that."

Janie called from the yard. "Shanna, is Katie all right?"

"She's fine, Miss Janie. You can come in if you want. She just got confused and hit her knee again."

Shanna opened the screen door to let Janie in, explained the situation and then walked over to where Simon stood near the kitchen counter, watching as Janie hugged Katie close.

"She'll be okay. She's been through a lot, Simon. Her stepfather—"

"Don't say it," Simon replied, his eyes bright. "I can't bear to think it."

Shanna could see the horror in his eyes. "Well, whether we want to think about it or not, sometimes children are afraid of adults. He beat her, Simon. And her mother didn't do anything to protect her. That's why her grandparents have full custody. Katie has come a long way but she's still got a long way to go."

"You don't think I'd—"

"I don't think any such thing and it was wrong of the boys to even suggest that to Katie since I warned them of such nonsense. She's only eight, but she wanted to come on this trip and after her grandmother agreed to come and watch out for Katie and help me with the others, I let her, thinking it would be good for both of them, thinking I could protect her. So this is my fault."

Simon shook his head. "It's not your fault. I just didn't know what to do when she got so upset."

"What did you do?"

"I told her it was okay and asked her to let me see if she was hurt. Honestly, I used the same technique I'd use with a scared animal. I let her adjust to my being here." He looked over at the little girl. "Then I tried to help her up and she started sobbing. I didn't know what else to do but try and calm her."

"You did the right thing. She's not used to being comforted, especially by men. She's with her grandparents now, and things are better. You didn't do anything wrong."

His skin went pale. "I hope the stepfather is out of the picture."

"He is, finally. But her mother left with him about six months ago—just up and left her child. Katie still has nightmares. I think her grandparents will have custody of her for a long time."

He swallowed, leaned against the counter. "Maybe you were right earlier. Maybe it is time I get out into the world. If for no other reason, to make sure children don't have to suffer like this."

Shanna's heart swelled with appreciation and thankfulness. "You can start by trying to help me with the seven I've brought here on this retreat, if you'd like."

He nodded his head. "What about Katie? I don't want her to be afraid of me."

"Just show her the same concern you showed her tonight and she'll be fine. I promise. She needs to see that adults can be gentle and loving."

He didn't look so sure. But he turned and walked over to where Katie sat. "Katie?"

The girl looked up at him. "Yes, sir?"

"I was wondering if you and the others would like to see where I work. Maybe tomorrow morning?"

Katie's eyes brightened at that. Then she looked at Shanna. "Would that be okay?"

"I think it's a great idea," Shanna said, knowing in the way the offer had rushed out that Simon was just as frightened as Katie. She nodded toward Simon. "Thank you."

He reached out to pull a strand of Katie's dark red hair away from her wet cheeks. "You'll be okay, Katie. As long as I'm around, no one will hurt you, you understand?"

Katie nodded. And smiled.

While Shanna blinked back tears and thanked God for this one small thing.

Chapter Five

Simon stared at the group of people standing on his back porch then wondered how his life had gone from peaceful and uncomplicated to overrun with kids of all shapes, colors and sizes. And one very persistent woman.

"Good morning," Shanna said, grinning at him through the screen door. "We're here for the tour."

"The tour?" Simon glanced at the clock. He'd barely had his coffee. He didn't do mornings.

Katie stepped forward, her long curly ponytail bouncing. "Remember, Mr. Simon. You promised me you'd show us how you make boots. You didn't forget, did you?"

Simon looked at Shanna, feeling helpless

in the innocence of that gentle reminder. How could he resist this adorable little girl? Or the adorable grown girl, her own dark hair falling around her shoulders, staring at him right now?

"Uh, no, I didn't forget. Just getting my bearings."

"What's that?" Katie asked through a giggle.

"He forgot," Brady said, sarcasm sharpening his frown. "And now, he's tap-dancing."

Katie looked at Simon's feet. "He's not even moving, Brady."

Brady rolled his eyes. "Can we just get on with this?"

Shanna gave Simon a questioning look. "Are you ready?"

"As ready as I'll ever be," he retorted. But he tried to smile when he said it. He sure didn't want to scare anyone else even if it was mighty tempting to shout his wrath to those teasing boys and watch 'em scatter.

Shanna gave him a once-over then said, "Okay, first—names. You know Brady and Katie. And you've seen Felix, Lavi, Pamela, Marshall and Robert. That's everyone.

Miss Janie stayed behind to clear away our breakfast dishes."

"Do we have to do this?" Marshall asked, his fingers moving through his burnished brown hair like a pair of desperate shears.

Simon felt pretty much the same way. He sure agreed to that suggestion. The sooner the better. "If you're not interested—"

Shanna clapped her hands. "Why don't you all sit down and let me have a word with Simon, to see what the rules are regarding a tour."

"We have too many rules," Felix said. He flopped down on the steps and put his head on his knees. "Why'd you get us up so early?"

"Rules for your own safety and good," Shanna said. "And we got up early because we have a busy day. We're going rafting this afternoon, remember?"

"That's the reason I came," the girl called Lavi said, glancing out at the water. "I love rafting. My mom and dad take us every summer."

"After the tour," Katie replied, taking Simon's hand in hers. "I'm ready."

"Katie come with us," Shanna said. "The rest of you stay put."

Groans everywhere. Simon wanted to groan, too. How could Shanna look so fresh-faced and ready to actually talk to other human beings this early in the day? Simon got up early, but he didn't talk to anyone until well after nine o'clock. And then only if he couldn't avoid it.

Shanna took him by the arm and held Katie's hand as she moved them both inside the cabin. "Simon, if you don't want to be bothered—"

"It's fine," he said, slanting his eye toward Katie. He couldn't disappoint her, not after scaring her so badly last night. He'd had a bad night just remembering what Shanna had told him about the little girl. "I'm ready and willing."

"What's the plan then?" Shanna asked, her blue eyes glimmering with a challenge. "Can they just walk through, or will you be able to demonstrate how you make a boot?"

"How about both?" he said, making it up as he went. He rarely allowed anyone in his shop. Little beads of sweat popped out on his backbone. "They don't need to touch anything and they need to listen and look. They can ask questions if they want, I reckon."

"Got it." Shanna turned, her hair doing a ribbon around her neck. She'd left it down this morning. He liked it that way. She looked young and carefree.

Simon watched her walk back out onto the porch and heard her issuing instructions to the kids. Katie stood there looking at Simon.

Nervous, he asked, "How ya doing, Katie?"

"Fine." She kept staring, her big green eyes reminding him of the moss growing on the rocks down by the river.

"Is something wrong?"

"I don't see any fangs, is all."

Simon started to tell her he took his fangs out at night, but decided he's traumatized the kid enough. "I don't have fangs. I'm actually a very nice person. I just like to work all the time."

"Miss Shanna says we need to take time to stop and smell the honeysuckle."

"Is that right?"

Katie bobbed her head. "It sure smells so good."

"Yeah, it does." He couldn't remember the last time he'd even noticed the honeysuckle blooms. Or the river. Or the azaleas and dogwoods. If he didn't have all those dated orders, he wouldn't even know the season of the year.

Shanna called out. "Simon, we're good to go now."

Katie took Simon's hand again. "I can't wait to see how you nail boots together, Mr. Simon."

Simon looked down at the little girl's hand in his, a lump forming in his throat as a painfully sweet sense of hope warmed his heart. Would his child have looked as cute as Katie?

He closed his eyes for a minute, pushing away his own pain as he remembered this child had been abused at the hands of another adult. What kind of man would hit a little girl? In spite of what she'd been through, in spite of how frightened she'd been last night, Katie was still so innocent and full of light and hope. This child wanted to be loved. Even Simon with all his cynicism and doubt could see that in the hopeful way she looked up at him, trusting him only because he'd promised her a tour of his work space. Trusting him, maybe because he's also promised her that while he was around, no one would harm her.

He'd stick to that promise, no matter his own pain.

He opened his eyes, his gaze colliding with Shanna's. She gave him one of her knowing smiles then waited for him to guide them to the shop out behind the cabin.

"Bootmaking is an art," Simon said, his voice raspy and awkward. He grabbed a funny-looking pair of pliers, gripping them like a lifeline.

Shanna nodded, silently encouraging him to keep talking. He sounded rusty and aged, as if he hadn't spoken so many words in a very long time. But his eyes grew dark and bright when he held up the pair of boots he'd been working on. Just seeing the rich, thick leather, Shanna could tell bootmaking was an art. Simon was an artisan. It showed in his eyes and in the way he handled the boot.

"If a bootmaker has return customers, then he's done his job," Simon continued. "That's the sign that he knows what he's doing and that the customer is pleased."

"Do you get return customers?" Blond-haired Robert asked, his big eyes widening.

"All the time," Simon replied, his fingers moving over the beautiful brown and gold leather. "This is the third pair I've made for this particular client. He favors this candle stitch. I can't take credit for the original idea, but I've done my own version of the original." He pointed to the inlaid gold leather that looked like a fire moving up the upper part of the boots. "I stitched these with glistening gold thread. Looks like real gold."

"That's one of Mr. Adams's trademarks," Shanna pointed out. "He always puts golden-colored soles on his boots."

Clearly impressed that she knew this, Simon grinned. "That's right."

He caused her to lose her breath. The man needed to grin more often.

"Shanna is correct. I like to burnish the soles. Makes 'em shiny and waxy. And I work hard on the vamps and shafts. One of my favorite designs and one that's requested a lot is the 'Heart of Gold' inlay. It features shimmering golden hearts on the uppers. Women love those."

He gave Shanna another grin. "Most women, that is."

"Why don't you make Miss Shanna a pair?" Katie asked, clapping her hands together. "She likes shoes."

Simon looked surprised. "Uh, I could do that. I'd just need to measure her foot."

"Do it, do it," Katie said. "She won't mind."

Soon, the others were chiming in. "C'mon, Miss Shanna."

"You don't have to—"

Simon grunted at Shanna, held up a hand then went to a long table and brought back two square sheets of parchment paper and a red pencil, along with a measuring tape.

"Take off your sandals."

Shanna lifted her eyebrows. "Excuse me?"

"I'm gonna measure you for a pair of boots. Take off your sandals."

Katie giggled in glee, then the chant went up again. "C'mon, Miss Shanna."

Shanna didn't want to disappoint the little girl, but she'd rather not force this on Simon. "You don't have to do this," she said to Simon under her breath.

"I want to."

She doubted that, but she removed her shoes.

"Put your right foot straight down on the paper," he said after placing one of the sheets at her feet.

Shanna did as he said then watched as he carefully traced her feet with the red pencil, leaving an outline that looked like a footprint. Then he did the same with her other foot. "One might measure slightly bigger than the other, but it'll work out."

Before he'd finished, he'd also taken measurements of her heel, what he called the high instep, the low instep (that tickled) and the waist—or middle of her foot, as he explained. His hand on her skin was warm and sure.

Lavi laughed at that. "I thought our waist was in our stomach."

"Your foot has a waist, too," he replied, concentrating on his work. He looked up at Shanna, his hand holding her foot. "You have tiny feet." His hand moved to the ball of her foot, his fingers sending little charges across her toes.

"I'm a size seven, but narrow."

"Yep, that's just about right." He stood, his dark blue eyes reminding her of the ashes in their smoldering campfire. "They'll fit like a glove."

Shanna's breath held tightly to her lungs while his eyes held tightly to her. They seemed locked together in time.

"Do they cost a lot?" Brady asked, breaking the spell. "Do you make a lot of money?"

Simon put down the traces and his pencil and measuring tape then clasped his hands together, clearly becoming more comfortable. "Not really. It takes me a whole work week—about forty hours—or sometimes longer—to make one pair of boots. I charge a lot because I have to put a lot into each pair. I make them to last a lifetime and I try to use as little equipment as possible, so that means mostly by hand. But, I can't complain. I make enough to keep me happy, I reckon."

"What if somebody wants a plain pair without all the fancy stuff?" Marshall asked, pushing at his round-frame glasses.

"I make that kind all the time," Simon replied. "Most folks want a good solid working boot. A lot of my clients are working men and women—ranchers, farmers, horse owners, people like that. Or they want a good pair of boots for church on Sunday."

Shanna glanced up at that remark. She'd never seen Simon in church. Did he have a pair of boots he reserved for Sunday? Or did he avoid church the way he avoided everything else?

"Why do people like boots, Mr. Simon?" Katie asked, her fingers dancing across the front of her lacy blue top.

Simon glanced at Shanna, his smile soft and sure now that he'd found his "bearing." "I think we all love cowboys—and cowgirls—heroes who are honorable and brave. Cowboy boots have been around for over one hundred and fifty years. That's a long time."

"I'll never be that old," Lavi said, her golden blond hair falling around her face. "And I don't have any boots like that. But my daddy's tattoos kinda look like some of your designs."

"Everybody should have a good pair of boots," Simon replied. "Some of my clients collect 'em." He touched her nose with his finger. "And, some of my clients also have tattoos."

"We aren't all loaded like your customers," Brady replied, jaded and not necessarily impressed. "That's what my mother tells my sister when she begs for a pair of your boots."

Simon nodded, a twist in his lips. "You don't have to buy a handmade pair. But if you do, they'll last you for a long, long time."

"Can we see some of the tools you use?" Shanna asked, still recovering from his hand holding her foot. She loved hearing

Simon explain things in his deep voice. He clearly came alive when he talked about his work. Maybe because his work kept his mind off his grief and pain?

"Sure." He held up the pliers again. "These are bullfrog pincers. They help me cut the leather." He turned and pointed to a bench. "This is one of my work benches. I mount the leather on this mold so I can get a good grip. And this crimping board is used to stretch and dry wet leather so it won't wrinkle when I put together a boot."

"How do you learn to make boots?" Pamela asked.

"You can train at a school or apprentice with some of the old-time bootmakers. There are still a few around. That's what I did."

"What made you decide?" Brady asked.

Simon sat silent for a minute then looked up at Shanna. "I…uh…saw a pretty girl wearing a pair of colorful boots with a long dress. They had roses on 'em. I asked her where she got 'em and she told me her parents had them handmade for her." He dropped his head. "I fell for the girl and I did research on bootmaking."

He looked up again and into Shanna's eyes. "Lost the girl, but found a new occupation."

Shanna couldn't look away. Was he talking about Marcy? Had his late wife been the reason he became such a craftsman?

"I love what I do," he said, as if he were truly trying to explain this to her and her alone.

Shanna gave him a soft smile, hoping he'd see that she understood. "Can we see some of your finished products?"

"Sure. I have a special wall full of finished boots. My brother and mother help me process the orders when I get behind, but for the most part, I'm on my own here. My customers know I don't get in a big hurry."

On his own amid these lovely creations, Shanna thought. That was a shame. He probably could use some help.

But he didn't want any help. She understood him a lot better now.

Amazing that a man could create such beautiful boots when his soul seemed so dark and gloomy. But she could see through that gloom into his heart. And she was pretty sure that battered and bruised heart was just like his boots.

Full of gold.

God had given Simon a rare talent.

And left him alone with that talent.

No wonder the man was shaken with having her and her seven wards around for a week.

But then, Simon wasn't the only one shaken by their time together. Shanna's heart went out to him. Being inside his studio and seeing firsthand what made him tick, what gave him strength, had helped her to see inside his heart and soul, too. And she prayed she could do or say something to bring him out of his shell so that his soul could shine again.

When the tour was finished, she turned at the door. "Thank you. I think they really enjoyed this."

"My pleasure." He held the door for her then said, "Hey, what kind of design do you want on your boots?"

Shocked, Shanna swung around. "You're

not serious about making me a pair of boots. I can't afford them, you know."

"Of course I'm serious and this pair's on me."

"I can't let you do that, Simon."

"I insist. It's a gift. Now what kind of design do you want?"

Touched and a bit rattled, she said, "I love sunflowers. But that heart-of-gold design sounded pretty too. Why don't you surprise me?"

"I'll do my best." And with that, he gave her a quick smile then shut the screen door. "Y'all come back any time."

Shanna had to smile at that. The bootmaker had made progress today. He'd actually opened up his world to a group of curious kids. And one very curious woman.

It was a start.

She couldn't wait to try on her new boots, but she figured it would be a long time before that happened.

Besides, this week wasn't over yet. His good mood might change. He'd probably be so glad to have them gone so he could retreat back into his own world. And he'd forget all about sunflowers and hearts.

And her, too.

Chapter Six

"Would you like to go rafting with us?"

Simon gave Shanna a questioning look. "You're asking me?"

"I don't see anybody else standing here."

It was afternoon now and he had yet to hit a stitch of work. This woman was seriously cramping his style.

Simon let out a grunt. "First, you convince me to open up my studio. Then I somehow wind up having lunch with y'all. And now you want me to go rafting? Afraid you'll lose one of the rug rats?"

She shook her head. "I'm not twisting your arm. I can handle these kids. They're all good swimmers and they know to keep their life vests on. We're doing the kiddy rapids, hardly a bump. And the water's only a foot or two deep in most places. I just thought you might have a good time."

Simon could picture her at the helm of a big yellow raft, shouting cute little orders to the kids. "You're a real adventuress, aren't you?"

"I like to live life to the fullest, yes."

He could see that life in the way her vivid eyes lit up whenever she was talking to one of the kids. He saw that life in her smile, her laughter, her every movement.

He envied that.

"I've got work to do," he said. "It's already Tuesday. The whole weekend went by and I'm getting behind."

Shanna was definitely a big part of that. She was a tempting distraction. This goofing-off stuff was new to Simon. Marcy used to drag him out to play, but he'd given all of that up after her death. He needed to turn around and get back to the grindstone. But he didn't turn around.

Shanna did the hands-on-the-hips thing, her gaze boring into him. "Don't you ever take a break and have fun?"

"My work is my fun." And it was his

livelihood, his salvation, his escape. So why wasn't he rushing back to that work?

"We're only going to be gone a couple of hours."

"And then you'll talk me into eating hot-dogs with you."

She held up two fingers. "I won't. Scout's honor. Besides, we're having pizza tonight. In town. At the Pizza Haus."

He wasn't going to eat pizza with her. Especially not in town. No way. But he didn't say anything to the contrary. "I can see you as a Girl Scout. All get-up-and-go, all valor and honor."

"And you have a problem with that?"

"No, I don't. But I can't go rafting with you this afternoon. I—"

"Have work to do. I get it." She lifted her arms in the arm, her hair falling in water-fall waves around her shoulder. "How can you resist all this sunshine and the wisteria scent on the breeze?"

Simon watched her, enjoying the way she held her head toward the warm sunshine, his breath slapping against his lungs.

He said yes.

But not because he couldn't resist spring or pizza.

He just couldn't resist her.

"I'm really glad you decided to come," Shanna said later as they helped the kids get into their life vests. "I needed to take two rafts and I was concerned with no adults being on the second one. Miss Janie can't go because of her bursitis and I couldn't find another volunteer when I asked at church last week."

He gave her a wry smile. "So I'm the designated adult?"

"I guess so. Can you handle it?"

He laughed. "My brother and I have been running the Hooch for years, sweetheart."

Shanna filed the *sweetheart* away to savor later, thinking he hadn't even realized he'd called her that. "The 'Hooch'?"

"I forget you're a Savannah-by-way-of-Texas girl. The Hooch is what all the locals call the Chattahoochee River. So don't worry. I know this river like I know the back of my hand."

"I'll hold you to that," she said. "We're only going down river as far as Knotwood.

Then after we eat at the Pizza Haus, Rick and Cari are going to drive us back out here in their two cars."

"Great. I'll never hear the end of this. And I'll never get home. Anything involving my family usually turns into a big, long and drawn-out event."

Shanna liked the twinkle in his eyes. "Are you sure? I don't want you to get all grouchy on me because I made you miss work. Or because your brother rags you."

He stared at her for a moment, his inky eyes making her insides go all mushy and jumpy. "If I act grouchy, it won't be because of work or my brother, let me tell you."

Not sure how to take that, she lifted her brow. "Do I make you uncomfortable, Simon?"

"You make me a lot of things," he retorted. Then he hurried over to help Katie put on her helmet and life vest. "And Katie rides with me," he called out.

Shanna turned to Janie, shrugging.

"That man says the oddest things," Janie said, her hand over her mouth. "I'm amazed he's practically spent the whole day with us."

"Me, too," Shanna said. "But look, Miss Janie, he's actually smiling. And the kids seem to like him."

Janie glanced over to where Katie was giggling at something Simon had said. "I hope Katie won't be a bother."

"Not at all," Shanna said. "She and Simon have gotten past their fear of each other, I believe."

The older woman nodded. "Katie adores him and let me tell you, that's a major step for her. She rarely takes to people she doesn't know, especially if she's scared of them."

"He was kind to her last night," Shanna replied. "They bonded—good for both of them."

"That little girl sure needs a positive male presence in her life. Her grandfather loves her, but he can't always keep up with her constant energy."

Shanna thought Simon would keep up, just to protect Katie. Maybe Katie was the reason he'd agreed to come on the rafting trip. He'd been so considerate of Katie since Shanna had told him some of the child's history. Shanna wondered what he'd say about her own history, but she put those dark thoughts out of her mind. She didn't like talking about her past.

"I hope the other kids behave around him," she said. "They admire his art, that's for sure."

"Teenagers have a way of putting people in their place," Janie said. "Maybe this forced togetherness is good for Simon, too."

"I think so," Shanna replied. She hoped so. "Are you sure you'll be okay here alone?" she asked Janie after checking her supplies.

"I'll be fine, honey. I plan to read out on the deck then take a nice nap. Lee said he might drive out and keep me company. I think he's getting lonely back at the house. We might even go fishing. We haven't done that in years."

"You both deserve a break. We'll watch out for Katie. I feel better, having Simon along."

"I think Katie does, too." Janie watched her granddaughter. "You know, children are very smart that way. Katie's attitude toward Simon speaks a lot about him. If she didn't like being around him, she'd sure let me know."

"He handled things with grace and patience last night," Shanna said. "But then, who wouldn't fall for Katie. She's adorable."

"I can't argue with that," Janie said, her smile full of hope. "This outing has helped her so much."

"We'll take good care of her, I promise." Shanna glanced around. "Okay, I think I have everything. And you have your phone. My cell will be on, so call if you need anything."

"I will." Janie went up onto the deck and sat down. She waved over to Katie. "Be sweet, Ladybug."

Katie and Simon got onto the big orange raft with a couple of the others then waved back.

And this time, they were both smiling.

"Well, look at you. Country's come to town."

Simon grinned up at Jolena. A friend to everyone, Jolena ran the local diner and was famous for her good old-fashioned soul food. "And look who came into the Pizza Haus. Don't you own a diner?"

"Yes, but my kids like pizza once a week." Jolena's dark eyes sparkled right along with the silvery beads on her long dreadlocks. "It's good to see you, Simon."

Simon had to admit being in town around people had turned out to be a pleasant surprise. "Shanna kind of roped me into chaperoning."

Jolena's gaze moved over the kids at the long table. "Shanna has a heart of gold. She loves teaching and she loves the Lord. She's a real sweetheart. Cari goes on and on about her."

Simon looked across to where Shanna was talking quietly with Pamela. The woman did have a way with teens. Even this rowdy bunch seemed to calm down around her.

"She's brave, I'll give her that," he said to Jolena.

Jolena touched his shoulder. "And so are you, my friend. You need to come into town more often. I still have the best pie on Knotwood Mountain, you know."

Simon closed his eyes. "Ah, I remember

pie." Then he opened them to find Shanna looking at him, her expression expectant and full of wonder. Did she like him just a little bit?

Tearing his gaze away, he turned back to Jolena. "My Ma brings me one of your pies each week."

"Your mother likes to spoil her boys, even if you are both grown men."

Simon had to agree with that. "She wants grandchildren, too. Maybe Rick and Cari can handle that."

"No reason why you can't be a daddy one day," Jolena said on a throaty chuckle. She eyed Shanna. "At least one young lady is available and apparently more than willing to be a mother."

"Are you suggesting…Shanna and me… become an item, Jolena?"

"Who? Me?" Jolena's chuckle ricocheted off the ceiling, causing several people to glance up. "I'd never think such a thing." She slapped Simon on the back. "I'd better go before my children call 911, looking for that pizza. Just think about it." She pointed toward Shanna.

"Yeah, right." Simon dropped his gaze

then lifted his eyes to get another look at Shanna. She'd gone back to talking to Pamela, but her gaze slammed into his for a couple of seconds. Then she looked back down.

Which gave him a perfect opportunity to observe her. She sure was pretty, but Jolena was right. Shanna's beauty came from within, even if that did sound like a cliché.

There was something to be said about old adages such as that. But was he ready to get close to another woman?

In some ways, Shanna was a lot like his deceased wife. Funny, pretty, caring, loving. But Marcy had golden blond hair and big green eyes. Shanna had those huge, deep blue eyes and that midnight dark hair. She looked nothing like his wife. But she sure had some of the same qualities. Those qualities had drawn Simon to Marcy.

Could he even think about another woman?

His brother Rick slinked into the empty chair next to Simon. "You're just full of surprises this week."

Simon knew it was coming but he tried to

stall his brother's keen sense of observance. "Oh, and why is that?"

"You haven't been into town since the Christmas Festival. In fact, I don't think you've left our place since Christmas."

"I've been busy," Simon said in his own defense. Didn't his brother get that?

"And now, you're eating spaghetti with a group of kids, comforting scared little girls, flirting with cute big girls and eating pizza at the Pizza Haus. Who are you and what have you done with my real brother?"

Rick's teasing was lighthearted, but it stung Simon back to reality. "I don't know," he admitted, being honest with Rick. "I should have stayed home. I need to be working."

"Maybe you need to be right here," Rick said under his breath, his expression serious. "You need this, Simon. Whatever made you come on the rafting trip, I'm glad. You look ten years younger."

Simon had to admit he felt younger, lighter, more relaxed. "It was just a trip down river, Rick."

"Maybe so," Rick said, waving over to

where Cari sat with Shanna. "Or maybe it was a journey that's about to change your life."

"Don't be so overly dramatic," Simon replied, trying to find the old bitterness and anger he used as his only shield.

But his armor didn't feel as strong now. Maybe because Shanna White had put a deep chink in his protective shield. Would that piercing also damage his already bruised heart? Did he really want to take that next step and find out?

Shanna looked up and smiled at him. And suddenly, Simon didn't want to be sitting across the table from her.

He wanted to be near her.

"I should have stayed home and worked," he repeated to his brother. "I don't think I'm ready for this, Rick."

Then he got up and went out onto the deck that overlooked the river, his mind swirling just as fast and swift as the tiny, gurgling current.

What am I doing? he asked himself. He felt as if he'd betrayed Marcy. He was caught between elation and agony, remembering one woman yet sitting across the table from another one, thinking about what it would be like to kiss *her.*

This is wrong, he thought.

But oh, how he wished it could be right.

Chapter Seven

Shanna watched Simon stalk out onto the deck, the sound of the screen door slamming shut jarring her out of her relaxed, happy mood.

"Excuse me, Pammie," she said, getting up. She walked over to where Rick sat staring at the door. "What's wrong with him?"

Rick twirled his straw in his drink, clinking ice cubes against the plastic cup. "You, I think."

Shanna sank down on a chair. "He's mad at me, isn't he? I shouldn't have insisted on him coming along with us all day."

"No, it's not that," Rick said, letting out a long sigh. "I think you scare him, Shanna.

You bring up all those memories he'd tried so hard to suppress."

"I shouldn't have pushed him," Shanna replied, glancing out toward the deck. "I'm bad about that—pushing people too far." She could see Simon's silhouette, the glowing yellow lights strung across the deck pitching him in shadows and light. "I like him, Rick. I only wanted him to let loose and have some fun."

"And he did," Rick said. "But he needs to process this whole week. Simon was never one to rush into anything and just getting him into town and here is a minor miracle. Give him some time."

Shanna still wished she'd gone on her first instinct. To leave Simon alone. "Should I go out there?"

Rick looked out to the porch. "I don't think so. He'd be polite to you, but right now he needs to think about what he's feeling. My brother tends to internalize everything so I'm sure he'll deal with this in his own time."

Shanna got up, thinking it was time to get the kids back to the cabin. "I'm sorry."

"Don't apologize for caring. He needs

someone besides our mother and me to bring him out of his self-imposed exile. And I think you might be just the person to do it." He shrugged. "I'm not so sure about how he'll react, but don't give up on Simon. He needs a friend."

"Thanks," she said. "Guess we'd better head back. We put all the rental equipment out on the landing behind the general store."

"I'll take care of getting it back inside," Rick said. "Don't worry about that."

"I appreciate your help," she said. Then she turned to the kids and clapped her hands. "Okay, time to load up, people. We need to get back for evening devotionals."

She saw Simon pivoting to come back in. He must have heard her. Her cell phone went off before she could say anything to him. "Hello?"

"Shanna, this is Lee Munson. I'm out at the camp with Janie and she isn't feeling good. I've called an ambulance. They're taking her back into town to the hospital right now. Can you meet us there?"

"I'm on my way," Shanna said, panic

gripping her heart. She hung up, glanced around. "Where's Katie?"

Simon hurried toward her when he heard her question. "She's right there with Pamela and Cari. What's wrong?"

Shanna pulled Rick and Simon close then motioned to Cari. "Janie is sick. Lee had to call an ambulance out to the cabin. I need to go to the hospital. But I can't take all these kids."

Simon took her by the arm. "I can take the kids back out and watch them until you get back."

Remembering her conversation with Rick earlier, she said, "I can't ask you to do that."

"I don't mind," he said. "I have to go back home anyway."

"And we can help," Rick replied, looking over at Cari. "Right?"

"Of course," Cari said. "You go to the hospital and check on Mrs. Munson. We'll get the kids home and settled in." She hugged Shanna. "Call us with news."

"What about Katie?" Shanna asked. "She'll want to know where her grandparents are."

"I'll make sure she's okay," Simon said. "I promise."

Shanna knew she could count on that promise, even if she couldn't count on the man for anything else. "Okay. Someone will need to drop me off at the hospital."

Rick nodded. "Cari can take you in her car. I'll drive some of the kids in my Jeep and if Simon doesn't mind, he can take the van I use for hauling rafts and canoes and bring the rest."

Simon gave Shanna one last look. "Don't worry, okay?"

"Okay." She grabbed his shirt sleeve. "Thank you so much."

Simon leaned close, giving her a quick hug. "Go on now. I'll try to distract the kids."

Shanna turned to the seven children now watching her with expectant faces. "I have to make a quick side stop, so Simon and Rick are going to drive you back to the cabin. I'll be there soon."

Brady looked doubtful but Shanna didn't have time to explain right now.

She turned back to Simon one more time. He gave her a soft smile but she saw the concern in his eyes. And she also saw the quiet strength that had been there all along.

Then she left, trusting in that strength as Cari drove her to the hospital.

Simon paced the tiny den of the rental cabin, wondering when Shanna would get home. He'd watched an animated movie with Katie while the bigger kids had played board games and listened to their ever-present iPods.

Now it was late and getting later. He'd sent Rick and Cari back to town to check on Janie and Shanna, and Katie had long since finally given in and gone to bed. The other kids were now watching a movie, most of them dozing, too.

But Simon couldn't sleep.

He kept remembering Katie's questions.

"Where's Miss Shanna? Where's my Grammy? Why isn't she here?"

"Uh, she had to go into town. She'll be back soon. They'll both be back soon."

He hoped. He wouldn't know how to handle anything else.

What would he tell the little girl if something had happened to her grandmother?

How did you tell a child such news?

He didn't want to remember Marcy's sickness and death, but he couldn't think about anything else right now. Long nights, holding her. Even longer nights staying in the hospital 24/7. And then, one horrible night when they'd taken her tired little body away and he'd sat staring at an empty bed.

Empty. That's the way he'd felt for so long now.

Then he thought of Katie and how she'd asked him to read her favorite book. The book her Grammy read to her every night. "The one that I brought in my suitcase. It's about Noah's Ark. He had a lot of animals on there, you know."

Simon had found the book and read it twice. Then he'd watched, amazed, as Katie's long lashes had winked and wobbled until finally they'd fluttered shut with all the softness of a butterfly's wings.

Oh, Lord, that kind of intense love could kill a man.

And he'd already died ten deaths over,

losing Marcy. He couldn't go through that again, not with such a sweet, innocent child as Katie and certainly not with such a sweet, caring woman as Shanna.

He felt trapped in a misty web of innocent longing. A little girl and a grown woman, doing him in simply by being themselves. Why did they have to show up on his doorstep, anyway?

Simon couldn't breathe. He glanced toward the bedroom where Katie slept, then turned to Brady. "Hey, I'm going out onto the porch to get some air. Listen for Katie, okay?"

Brady nodded and waved a hand then went back to watching the high school musical blaring across the screen.

Pamela looked at Brady then said, "I'll listen for her too, Mr. Simon."

Simon hit the back deck with a shuddering breath, taking in air in large, heavy gulps. How had he become so emotionally tangled in this ragtag band of campers?

Because of Shanna and the way she made him laugh, made him shake his head in wonder, made him so lonely he wanted to scream.

Shanna had a way with people. The woman probably communed with animals, too, since she seemed to love them as much as she loved children. Katie had told him all about how Miss Shanna pointed out the birds and named them. She'd even looked for bears and foxes, too. And even old Shiloh had fallen for her at first sight.

And maybe you did, too, Simon thought, trying to block that way of thinking before the words even popped into his head.

"No," he said into the night. "No. I can't do this. I won't do this." They'd all be gone soon, back to their own worlds. And he'd go back to his peace and quiet and solitude.

And a shattering loneliness.

It's only been a few days, he reminded himself. Things would get back to normal next week. And next time his infernal well-meaning brother rented this cabin, Simon would make sure he steered clear of any interlopers.

Bracing his hands on the deck's sturdy railing, Simon closed his eyes and listened to the gentle, never-ending gurgle of the river down beyond the trees. That sound had always been a part of his life. It soothed him, refreshed him and gave him a sense of peace. But now, he needed more.

God, I know I haven't talked to You very much. Not in a long, long time. But I'm asking You to wipe these thoughts of Shanna out of my head.

Simon had forgotten how to pray, really. So he didn't expect an answer. God hadn't given him any good reasons why his wife had to die so young. And he was pretty sure God wouldn't give him any relief for this agony piercing his soul tonight.

But, oh, how he longed to feel that connection with the Lord again. He'd so believed in God when Marcy was alive. Because she'd been a godsend to him.

And then, she was gone. Taken too soon.

Why should God listen to Simon now? And why should Simon turn back to God now? Would it matter?

He felt a warm touch on his arm and jumped. "What?"

"It's me," Shanna said, stepping back. "I'm sorry. Brady told me you were out here."

Appalled that he'd snapped at her, Simon

dropped his hands to his side. "I am. I mean, I just stepped out to get some air. I didn't hear you drive up."

She ran a hand through her hair then crossed her arms over her stomach. "Thanks. You can go home now."

Simon felt awful for being so grouchy. It wasn't her fault that he was all twisted up inside, that his soul singed with this burning pain. "How's Mrs. Munson?"

"She's okay. They thought she was having a heart attack, but they decided it was just indigestion. She's not used to eating so much junk food. Anyway, Mr. Munson insisted she go home tonight and sleep in her own bed."

"That's good. I'm glad it wasn't serious."

"Me, too. I guess Mr. Munson will come and get Katie tomorrow. They don't think she should stay out here without one of them."

"We could take care of her," he said, wishing he could take back the words the minute they'd slipped out. He didn't need to get any more involved.

Shanna looked up at him, the moonlight

glistening in her eyes like white flowers on water. "Look, Simon, I appreciate all that you've done, but you don't have to help anymore. I'm used to dealing with kids and believe it or not, this bunch isn't all bad."

Simon leaned toward her, thinking it was awfully nice of her to offer him an out. Was this the answer to his prayers? Did God want him gone so much that He'd send an answer that quickly?

Or did Shanna want him gone that much?

He pushed back against the deck. "I've made a mess of this."

"I don't know what you mean."

"Yes, you do. I'm bitter and mad and I'm not very good around people. I've always been the quiet older brother." He looked down at his boots. "It's just that you came rushing into my life and...I can't think, I can't work."

She gave him a feminine frown. "I said you're free to go."

He grabbed her then, pulling her into his arms. "No, Shanna, I'm not free to go. I can walk away and go inside my house and close the door, but then I'll still be thinking of you and Katie and Brady and the Munsons and all the rest. They all mean something to me." He shook his head. "Lavi was so cute tonight, telling me she got in trouble at school when another girl made fun of her dad's tattoos. She's like a little lioness, defending her daddy's honor. They've all got a story to tell. You're right, they're not bad kids." He pulled back to stare down at her. "And I don't want to think about what they've been through. I don't want to care, I don't want to hurt. Do you understand that?"

The glistening in her eyes turned from a reflection of moonlight to shimmering tears. "I understand better than you'll ever know, Simon." She tore away and turned her back. "So just go."

But he didn't go. He tugged her back around and lifted her chin. Then he kissed her, his lips grazing her face for just a breath before he gave in and touched his mouth to hers. And with that touch, he felt his heart caving and crashing and falling into a waterfall of confusion at her feet.

He would never be free again. But that thought didn't scare him nearly enough to make him walk away.

Chapter Eight

Shanna stood on the deck, talking quietly to Lee Munson on the phone. It was early and she didn't want to wake the others yet. She needed some quiet time.

"No, really, Mr. Munson. Please let Katie stay. If she gets homesick or has any problems, I'll make sure we get her home. But she loves being out here and I think it's done her a world of good."

"I don't want her to be a problem, Shanna. You have enough keeping up with the older kids. Janie feels pretty low, abandoning you this way."

"I'm okay," Shanna said, trying to reassure the older man. "Rick's mom, Gayle, is coming out today to help. It's her usual day off from the general store and she always comes out to the river on her days off. So see, we have things under control. She'll make a great chaperone."

"Only if you're sure."

"I'm very sure." She was sure about this, but not sure about the man living next door. And she didn't dare look toward Simon's cabin or shop. She needed Katie around to keep her mind off Simon and that life-changing kiss he'd planted on her last night. "I'll stay in touch. Tell Miss Janie to rest, okay?"

She closed her phone then looked out at the river. Yesterday had been near perfect. The weather warm and balmy, the river glistening and beautiful, and Simon seemed to have had fun. He'd smiled and laughed and frolicked just like a big kid. He'd looked young and happy.

What a difference a day could make.

Somewhere between the rafting and the pizza, Simon had realized he was way out of his comfort zone. He didn't want to be around Shanna and the seven campers. He didn't want to laugh and frolic and... live. And even though he'd kissed her as if he really *wanted* to be around her, she knew that kiss had been a means of trying to end whatever seemed to be developing between them. He'd gotten her out of his system and now he was back to being the reclusive bootmaker.

It shouldn't matter that every time the man was around, her heart did strange little dances of joy and anticipation. It shouldn't matter that she had no business thinking about him, wondering why he couldn't let go and live again. And really, it was none of her business.

Shanna knew all about hiding away while you tried to hide your pain. She'd done that for years herself. But then, Christ had come into her heart and life had changed for her. Maybe Simon needed to remember that he wasn't alone. God was before him, in him and behind him.

But grief could hide such things.

The cabin door opened and Pamela came out, bleary-eyed, with Katie by her side. "She woke up crying. I told her I'd find her grandmother."

Shanna bent down and took Katie in her arms. "It's okay. Your grandmother was tired last night, so Grandpa Lee took her home to rest in her own bed. If you want to go home, I'll take you. But Grandpa Lee said you could stay out here with us if you want."

Katie gulped back a sob and wiped her eyes. "Is today the day we go fishing?"

Shanna grinned big. "Yes. You remembered! Right after breakfast, we'll go down to the shallow part of the river and fish. You'll be able to see minnows swimming all around your water shoes."

Katie wiped at her nose. "Can I stay for that?"

"Of course you can. And if you feel better by then, you can stay as long as you want."

"Okay." Katie smiled again. Then she looked over at Simon's cabin. "Mr. Simon said he'd show me how to bait my hook."

Shanna wasn't so sure about that. "Honey, he might have to work. We kept him out an awfully long time yesterday. So don't be disappointed if he can't go fishing with us, all right?"

Katie appeared crushed but she nodded her head. "May I have some juice?"

"I'll get her some," Pamela said. "C'mon, Katie."

Shanna let out a sigh as the two girls headed back into the cabin. "I'll be in to start breakfast in a few minutes."

She heard a door slamming across the way, followed by a "woof." Shanna closed her eyes, willing herself to go straight into her own cabin. She didn't want to look over and see Simon and his dog. She needed to put any thoughts of her neighbor out of her mind. Katie needed her attention now. These kids needed her. Simon didn't.

"Breakfast," she whispered to herself. Then she whirled and went inside.

Simon followed Shiloh's woof of excitement then watched as Shanna hurried inside her cabin before he could even wave.

Did he blame her for high-tailing it away from him?

He'd told her he couldn't handle things then he'd kissed her.

How dumb was that? He'd really messed up this time.

He looked down at his brother's hopeful dog. "No," Simon said. "We are not going to play all day. No, sir. We've got things to do. Boots to make. Orders to ship."

Shiloh whimpered, his nostrils flaring toward the other cabin. The dog's big eyes lifted toward Simon.

"I don't care if you smell bacon frying."

The dog hung his head in defeat then strolled away.

Simon knew the feeling. But he had to get back on track. That kiss had changed things. Instead of getting Shanna off his mind, that kiss had only made him want to be around her even more.

But he wouldn't torment himself with these thoughts. He'd just march into his workshop and get the job done. He'd put the woman next door out of his mind.

Even if he did smell biscuits baking right along with that bacon frying.

Flowers. Simon worked with the bright yellow leather he'd dyed earlier in the week. He should be working on that pair of buttery brown boots ordered by a famous Hollywood starlet. And she'd probably wear them with a too-short skirt and bleached-blond hair to match the yellow lightning strike design she'd requested when he'd fitted her months ago.

Instead he was working on this pair of boots—for a woman who'd come marching across his heart and left her own boot print in less than a week. He'd worked most of the night on the boots for Shanna. Not exactly the best way to get her off his mind.

The white flower design, made from thin strips of leather that had to be skived—scraped with a special knife—would be sewn as inlay across the front and back quarters of the size seven boots. He'd put the flowers over the famous heart of gold emblem he used on a lot of his boots, making it look as though the blossoms were spilling out of the gold hearts. He'd give them a mesh inlay so Shanna could wear her boots in the summer.

Summer.

Yellow and white flowers blooming in a field.

Children splashing down in the river.

Walking through a meadow of wildflowers with Marcy.

Marcy was dead. Summer was over. Shanna was here.

But the image of Shanna wearing these boots stayed with him, enticing him to keep working. He stopped stitching and stretching, his head lifting at the sound of voices echoing out over the trees.

Shanna was alive and well and just out of his reach.

Simon had promised Katie he'd show her how to fish.

But he had work to do.

He tried going back to the intricate flower design, working with the pattern he'd created late last night.

"She might not want these boots," he reminded himself. He refused to dwell on that. They were a gift, plain and simple. He'd promised her, and he lived up to his promises.

And he'd make sure these boots were one of a kind.

A girlish giggle floated through the open windows.

He missed a stitch.

Simon stared down at his pattern then looked at the beginnings of the flowers taking shape, the smell of leather like oxygen to him. But suddenly, he couldn't breathe.

He got up and stalked across the workshop and out the door. If he didn't do something right now, he would ruin these boots.

Shanna looked up to find Simon standing up on the bank, fishing equipment in his hand and a black scowl on his face.

Did she dare wave?

Did she dare breathe?

She swallowed, willing herself to be calm and still. If the man sensed fear, he'd probably pounce like a big cat. But the memory of his gentleness last night, the memory of his lips hitting against hers, caused her to take in a breath that shuddered all the way down her body.

"Look!" Katie shouted, causing Shanna to drop her fishing pole. "It's Mr. Simon. He came. He came!"

"He's two hours late," Brady said on a snarl.

And what was his problem? Shanna wondered. The kid had been as surly as the man now approaching them. Maybe it was just the entire male species—and people thought women got moody. Hah!

Pamela looked over at Brady, her big blue eyes going dark. "He does have a job, Brady."

"I'm not talking to you, am I?" Brady shot back. He tugged at his pole. "This is lame. I'm tired of fishing."

Shanna watched as he stalked off. "Don't go too far."

He didn't look back. Pamela looked down at her pole, her expression bordering on crushed.

Felix rolled his eyes then started snickering. "Marshall, you should rig Brady's pole and make him think he caught something."

"Good idea," Marshall said, his impish grin spreading.

"Hold on," Shanna said, stopping him. "We're not going to do that kind of stuff, remember? We talked about bullying and playing tricks on people."

"You are so not fun, Miss Shanna," Marshall said, but he went back to his place on the bank. "Brady's just lovesick anyway."

Shanna didn't know what to make of that one. And she couldn't chalk up that ailment for Simon's condition since he looked pained to be here. With her.

"Hi," she said, hoping she sounded casual.

"Hi," he said on a grunt.

"You didn't have to come down here."

"Yes, I did. I couldn't concentrate."

"I'm sorry we're disturbing you."

Katie ran up and hugged Simon's legs. "Mr. Simon, I caught the tiniest fish. Wanna see? I have to throw him back but we put him in a bucket of water so I could watch him swim around." She waited, then tugged at his arm. "Are you coming?"

Simon dropped his gear. "Sure I'd like to see." He kept his eyes on Shanna until she had to look away.

Was he trying to burn a hole of disapproval right through her? Maybe he blamed her for that kiss. But he started it.

Shiloh came rushing down the bank, his bark indicating he was happy to be here even if his keeper wasn't.

Simon allowed Katie to drag him down to the shore. Together, they bent over the bucket to stare at Katie's treasure, his dark hair a sharp contrast to the girl's red curls. She watched as Simon patiently showed Katie how to put a worm on her hook, the sight causing Shanna to close her eyes and ask for restraint.

"You have to be careful. You don't want the hook to go into your skin," he said. "Are you scared of worms, Katie?"

"No," she said, shaking her head, her curls bouncing. "My Grandpa said they won't hurt me. But they sure are slimy."

Shanna had often longed for a family of her own and if she ever had a husband and a child, she hoped they'd look a lot like Simon and Katie did now. But that notion only reminded her that she had no business even thinking such things. That train of thought would only bring her more heartache.

And especially around a man as tempting as Simon Adams. What was wrong with her anyway? Shanna knew that happy endings were the stuff of make-believe and fairy tales. Reality was messy and painful and unpredictable. And so was he. That should be reason enough for her to put pretty day-dreams out of her head.

Getting back on track, she did a head count out of habit. Everyone was here even if they were getting restless. Why weren't the big fish biting?

Pamela glanced off toward where Brady sat on a bench. "Miss Shanna, can I take a break?"

Shanna looked at Brady then back to the girl. "I guess so. Don't go far."

Pamela made a beeline to Brady. Well, that explained that. She'd have to watch those two.

Marshall and Felix giggled and whispered. Robert sat off on the deck by himself, completely absorbed in catching a small bass he'd seen swimming near there.

Lavi rolled her eyes and threw out her line for the tenth time in ten minutes. "I can't get my cork in the right spot," she complained. But as usual, Lavi did it with a sweet smile. The preteen loved to fish.

"Nice day," Simon finally said, his scowl still intact. He reserved his best smiles for Katie, apparently.

"We've had good weather all week."

"Halfway there."

"You mean, we'll be gone Saturday afternoon? I guess you're counting the minutes."

"I didn't mean it like that, no. I just meant the week is halfway gone."

"And next week, you can get back to normal."

"I don't think I'll ever get back to normal."

She glanced over at him, ready to send him her own scowl. But his features had softened and shifted. The man almost looked pleasant, which threw her off completely. Simon was like a spring rainstorm—all thunder and lightning one minute, then gentle and refreshing the next. Would she ever understand him?

"I don't know what to say to you, Simon."

"Then don't talk. Let's just enjoy this fine spring day."

"If you say so."

He checked on Katie's line then leaned close. "I'm sorry I was a bear last night. You're a bit overwhelming."

"I'm just me," she replied, still stinging

from his mixed signals. "I'm here to help these kids, nothing more."

"I like you," he retorted, ignoring her declaration. "I do." He seemed so proud of that declaration.

"I get that. I like you, too. We don't have to take it any further than that. So just relax, okay. The only thing I'm trying to hook is a fish or two."

"Good."

"Good."

They went into silence, not a comfortable silence, but at least they were on speaking terms again, even if they weren't actually speaking. A soft breeze whispered through the trees and rippled the clear water. The rocks on the river bottom glistened and winked while schools of fish swam by in perfect symmetry. The sun was high in the sky and the earth was traveling around that sun.

Shanna decided she really didn't have anything to complain about.

Then everything happened at once.

Katie caught a fish, her squeal of delight echoing over the water.

Shiloh started barking and heading for the river, hoping to get in on the fun.

Marshall and Felix started roughhousing and both fell into the river. Shiloh went in after them.

Robert jumped up and went around the dock to get a better angle on his elusive bass. But he knocked the can of worms into the river as he went by.

And Lavi lifted her line high and got it tangled in a weeping willow. Then she dropped her pole and called out, "Miss Shanna, Brady and Pamela are gone."

Chapter Nine

Shanna let go of her own pole then turned to search the surrounding area. “Where did they go, Lavi?”

Lavi tried to yank her fishing line. “I didn’t see them. I don’t know.” She shrugged. “But I do know they broke one of your rules. We’re not supposed to leave without you.”

Simon saw the concerned expression on Shanna’s face then helped Katie get her fish off the hook. Katie held the squirming brim then dropped him in her bucket. “That’s a big one.”

“Katie, sit right here, okay?” Simon told the little girl. Then he headed over to Shanna. “The boys are fine down in the water with that mutt of mine. Let ’em be.

I'll go look for Brady and Pamela. You take care of Katie—and help Lavi get her line untangled before she falls in, too."

Shanna nodded and scanned the woods again. "How did I not see this? Brady and Pammie—an item. I'm clueless."

"You've had a lot on your mind," he said, giving her a reassuring smile. "Try not to worry."

"Just go and find them, please?" Shanna retorted, her hand on her forehead. "I'll get everybody else back to the cabin. I've had enough of fishing for one day."

Simon saw the fatigue in her eyes. She tried so hard to make things right for everyone. He had to wonder who was around to make things right for her. But then, he'd been so preoccupied with trying to avoid her he'd failed to even consider that Shanna might have her own burdens to bear.

Wondering where Brady and Pamela could have gone, Simon thought back to when he'd been a teenager with raging hormones. If Brady and Pamela had something going, they would do anything to find some time together. And that could lead to all sorts of problems and temptations.

Simon stomped through the woods, the scent of wisteria and honeysuckle assaulting his senses. Spring was a perfect time to bring out all the lovesick people. Maybe that's why he'd been acting just about as addled as poor Brady. He hadn't even noticed the flora and the fauna until Shanna had shown up. He noticed a lot of things now, however. Like her eyes, her hair, her smile. Her moods. The woman was mostly happy all the time. But she wouldn't be happy if he didn't find those kids.

He searched the rental cabin first, but the place was empty and quiet. Then he moved on to one of the main trails that followed the river. He didn't hear whispers or heavy breathing but that didn't mean the two MIA teens weren't up to something. Simon had lived in these woods all of his life and he had pretty good ears.

The place was silent. Too silent.

He whirled back toward his cabin and workshop, wondering if they'd found a secret spot where they could have some private time. The big family cabin was unlocked—he never locked the place—but no one was inside.

He glanced toward his workshop. He'd shut the door but he didn't remember locking it. Shiloh usually barked to beat the band if anyone approached by foot or in a vehicle. But then, Shiloh had been just as distracted lately as Simon.

When he heard a feminine giggle coming from inside, Simon hurried up to the back porch of the big barn and carefully opened the screen door.

Voices echoed out into the main studio. Were they in the storage closet?

Simon didn't bother staying quiet. He marched across the wooden floor and yanked open the big oak door.

And found two red-faced teens all cuddled up on a big unopened supply box.

"How y'all doing in here?" he asked, reminding himself that he was young once.

Brady shot up. "We…uh…were just talking."

Simon looked from Brady to Pamela. "Yeah, I'll just reckon."

How to handle this?

He said a quick prayer then settled down against an old table. "Look, I know all about young love—"

"We're just friends," Brady said, his face turning apple-red.

Pamela glared up at him. "I thought you said—"

"I didn't say anything," Brady replied, giving her a warning look.

Simon rubbed his temple with two fingers. "Okay, here's the deal. Brady, you're at least three years older than Pamela, right?"

"Two," they both responded.

"Okay, two. That's a big difference, all things considered. And the rule was you're supposed to stay with your chaperone at all times, right?"

"Right," Brady replied, looking guilty. "We got bored. We wanted to do something besides fish."

"Uh-huh. I get that."

Pamela stared crying. "Am I in trouble? Are you gonna call my mom?"

"Not up to me," Simon said. But if he were in charge, he'd do just that. "You broke a rule so I'll let Miss Shanna decide about how to deal with this." Then he shot them what he hoped was a stern look. "But I do have a beef with y'all coming into my studio without my permission. I believe Miss Shanna told y'all this place was off limits."

"Yes, sir," Pamela said, her big eyes filling with tears again. "I'm sorry."

"It's my fault," Brady said, lowering his head. "I talked her into sneaking away with me."

Pamela sniffed. "I wanted to."

"Simon?"

Shanna's voice lifted over the trees.

He looked at the two scared kids. "Don't move. I'll be right back."

He hurried to the back door. "In here, Shanna. I found 'em."

She rushed up the steps, her expression full of woe. "Your mother's here. She's taking care of the others."

Simon nodded and motioned toward the storage room. "They're in there."

Shanna pushed past him then took in the situation. The expression on her face changed from aggravated to embarrassed. "Brady, what's going on?"

"Nothing," Brady said. "We just...like each other."

Pamela sniffed again then looked up at him, hope coloring her eyes. "We do?"

Brady seemed fascinated with his sneakers. "Yeah, sorta."

Shanna shot Simon a look that told him he fit into the same category as Brady—the non-commitment category.

"I've given them a lecture," he said, hoping she'd cut him—and them—some slack. "I'll let you take it from here." He looked back at the kids. "I'll go help my mom."

"Thank you," Shanna said. She turned to Brady and Pamela. "Let's go sit outside and have a talk."

Simon waited for them then followed, this time making sure he locked things up tight. Watching as Shanna led the mortified teens to a picnic table, Simon wondered how anyone survived parenthood. He was beginning to have a whole new appreciation for his parents. And for Shanna White.

"Look, it's okay to like each other," Shanna told the two frowning teenagers. "But you're both still very young. You need to set boundaries. Remember, we talked about this after one of our devotionals."

"We just wanted to be alone," Brady said, his defensive tone causing his voice to squeak. "Felix and Marshall were giving Pammie a hard time."

"I understand that," Shanna replied, remembering the angst and agony of first love. "But you didn't have permission to leave the group. That's for your protection. I promised your parents I'd take care of y'all. I don't want them to be disappointed in any of us."

"We didn't do anything wrong, Miss Shanna," Pamela said, glancing over toward Brady. "We only got to know each other better this week."

"That's nice and I think it's good that you've become close. But Pammie, Brady is older. Your mom might not want you hanging around with an older boy."

"My mom never notices what I do," Pamela shot back. "She's always out with her friends or working."

Shanna's heart hurt for the girl. She needed some serious adult guidance. No wonder she'd skipped school and got caught for petty theft. "Honey, your mom supports you and your brother with her salary. She works hard."

"And she parties hard, too," Pamela shot back. "Brady understands me. His mom is always working, too."

Shanna took a deep breath. She sure remembered the years of neglect she suffered before her aunt took her in. She'd made peace with her own wayward mother, but it had not been an easy peace, and now it was too late for her and her mother. Because of that, she wanted to teach these troubled teens how to deal with life better than she had.

"Single mothers have to work," she said. "My dad left us when I was real young. And my mother had to work very hard to take care of us." So hard that she died way too young.

"But I bet she loved you," Pamela said. "I bet she put you first. My mom tries, but she's always so stressed."

Shanna decided honesty might work best here. "I'm not so sure my mother did put me first, honey." She wouldn't mention the stepfather who'd whipped her and verbally abused her. And she wouldn't mention that her mother had never stood up for her. Or that her mother had left with that man, choosing him over her in the same way Katie's mom had chosen a man over her child. "My mother had a lot of problems when I was growing up." Those problems had eventually destroyed her. And so did the man she loved.

"What did you do?" Pamela asked, her head up now.

Shanna said a silent prayer. "I was too young to do a whole lot. I…I got taken away when I was a teen. My aunt became my legal guardian and I lived with her until I went to college."

"I wish I could live with someone who cares," Pamela said.

Brady lowered his head. "My mom cares. She's just so messed up. She blames everyone else for things. But sometimes she brings it all on herself." He looked up at Shanna. "But I love her. She's always tried to take care of me."

"And she's still trying," Shanna said. "Your mom stood by you when you vandalized Cari's place, remember?"

"She blamed Cari—said she was trying to turn me against her. Cari was just trying to help me."

"And you and Cari are still close, right?"

"Yes, ma'am. My mom's gotten a little better about that."

"That's because of you, Brady. She loves you enough to trust that you'll love her in return and do the right thing. It's all about respect."

Pamela smiled over at Brady. "He told me that same thing."

"Really?" Shanna was surprised. Maybe Brady had been listening to some of his adult mentors all along. "That's good. You have to respect your parents even if you don't always like how they treat you. Acting out won't help things." Then because it needed to be said, she leaned close and added, "And Pammie, having a boyfriend is cool and nice, but if you take things too far you'll have a whole new set of problems. That's all about respect, too."

Brady looked over at Pamela. "She's saying I should respect you, not make you do anything you don't want to do."

"Would you?" Pamela asked. "I mean, would you still like me if—"

Brady stared at his feet then looked back at Pamela. "Yes, I'd still like you, no matter what."

The girl sat straight up, as if a weight had been lifted off her shoulders. "You're not just saying that because Miss Shanna is here, are you?"

Brady shook his head. "Cari's talked to me about the birds and the bees, things like that." Then he shrugged. "It's just hard sometimes."

"Yes, it is," Shanna said, reaching across to touch his arm. "But you have to be strong, Brady. You have to learn self-control and respect. Do you understand what I'm asking?"

"Yes, ma'am. Can we go now?"

Shanna decided she'd lectured enough for one day. "Yes, but if you two sneak off like that again, you won't be able to come on any more church retreats, understand? I had to get special permission to bring y'all out here. I'd be in trouble right along with both of you if anything bad happened."

"I'm sorry, Miss Shanna," Pamela said,

getting up to hug Shanna. "Don't make me go home yet."

"I won't, honey. You know I'm always here if you need to talk to me, okay?"

"Okay."

"And you, too, Brady. Always."

Brady gave her a curt nod. "Thanks."

Shanna breathed a long sigh of relief as she followed them back to their cabin. "We're having hamburgers for dinner. Y'all go in and wash up. We'll go for our afternoon hike before dinner, then it's evening devotionals afterward, okay?"

They nodded in unison.

Shanna looked up to find Simon standing on the back deck watching her. He gave Brady and Pamela a solemn look then smiled as she stepped up onto the porch. "You okay?"

"I think so." She came to stand beside him, her gaze taking in the pines and blue spruce trees. Off in the forest, a lone dogwood's blossom shone bright white against the dense foliage. "Remind me to never volunteer for this again."

"You don't mean that, do you?"

She shook her head, touched that he

seemed so serious "Not really. I want to make a difference with them. But they're just kids. I want them to understand that I've been there, you know?"

"I don't know," he said, stepping closer. "Why don't you tell me—about you? I'd like to know about your life, Shanna."

Shanna looked over at him, her heart beating against her ribs like a trapped bird. "No, you don't want to know," she said. Then she turned and went inside the cabin.

Chapter Ten

Surprised, Simon couldn't move. He couldn't even go after her. What did she mean by that?

Of course, he wanted to know. But did she *want* him to know? He thought back over the last few days. Days of watching her, getting to know her, seeing her eyes go bright, hearing her pretty laughter hitting like wind chimes against the walls of his resistance. He'd seen her doctor damaged knees, kiss away little tears, heard her talking with authority and firmness when one of the kids tried to pull one over on her. And he'd seen her abiding faith in every action and reaction.

He was immediately attracted to the way she embraced life, even though he'd been terrified to let go and follow her. And never once in all of that had he stopped to consider that she might be here with these kids because of the grief in her past, because of some secret place inside herself that she was trying to heal. In spite of what she'd told him, Shanna didn't show any outward signs of dwelling on her childhood pain. Maybe because she was so good at hiding it?

Now he felt like one big, shallow oaf for being so self-centered and demanding and…downright mean. When had this become all about him, anyway? This youth retreat was all about God's healing love, something Simon had avoided for years. What right did he have to judge or question? He'd been locked away from the horrors of the world, locked away in his own grief and pain.

Simon looked up at the blue heavens, his hands gripping the broad beam of the railing. "Boy, Lord, when You send a wake-up call, You really send it. I hear You loud and clear. I've been holed up here so long I've forgotten how to be compassionate toward other people."

Maybe he had buried his heart with his wife, but that didn't mean he had to stop breathing, right? When he thought about what little Katie had been through and how much that had bothered him, he could only imagine what Shanna might have suffered. Could it be just as bad?

And yet she greeted each day with a smile, she sang hymns of praise and thanks. She went out of her way to help others. And all the while, she had her own pain behind that sunny, sure disposition.

And that not only bothered him, it made him so angry he wanted to hit the railing and cry out to God. Why did bad things happen to innocent people?

And why had he pushed everyone around him away because he was so bitter? Marcy had been a gift, a wonderful, colorful, loving gift. A gift he didn't really deserve. But God had His reasons for taking that gift. Simon had focused on the loss, not the time he'd had with Marcy.

He saw it all in such a different light now.

A blinding light of reality gripped him in its shining honesty. He'd been looking at

Shanna as a distraction, and for that reason, he'd resisted that distraction. He had wanted only to wallow in his pain and his regret and his misery.

But what if Shanna was a second chance for a gift? A gift of a friend who could make him laugh and breathe and live life to the fullest, to embrace his faith again and become a part of humanity again? What if he looked at this as an opportunity rather than an intrusion?

Simon followed the wind as it teased the trees and caused some nearby wisteria blossoms to rain down all around him, their scent fresh now and renewed. The woods looked deeper and greener, the blooming flowers coming alive with such force Simon had to close his eyes.

And in that moment, his heart seemed to burst open with such a sweetly intense longing he bent over and templed his hands together to contain it.

He thought of part of a long-forgotten verse from Scripture.

Remember, O Lord, Your tender mercies....

Then he prayed, in earnest, in hope and

in forgiveness. Mostly, he prayed for Shanna and thanked God for sending her to him.

Shanna stood at the big wide window, her gaze caught on the man standing out on the deck. Was Simon okay? It looked as if he were deep in prayer. She almost went to him, but something held her back. He lifted up then, his hands falling to his side, and turned and looked straight into her eyes.

Then Gayle called out. "Shanna, dinner's all set up. The girls and I sliced tomatoes and put cheese and pickles on a plate in the freeze. We have chips and cookies. All we have left is grilling the burgers when we get back from our walk. Wanna rally the troops?"

Shanna turned away, just for an instant. "Yes. I'll be right there."

When she turned around, Simon was gone.

Gayle came over to her. "Katie's asleep. I can stay with her. Will you be okay with the others on the afternoon hike?"

"I'll be fine," Shanna said, thinking a nice long hike would get her mind off of Simon. "You don't mind staying here?"

"Not at all. It's always nice to take a break. And I'll see if I can wrangle Simon to help grill the burgers."

"No, don't do that."

Shanna wished she hadn't shouted that out. Now Gayle and some of the older kids were eyeing her with sharp surprise. "I'm sorry. I mean, we don't need to bother Simon about every little thing. He has to work."

Gayle drew her close. "Oh, my, has he been rude to you? That boy—"

"No, he hasn't been rude at all. I just don't want to disturb him again."

Gayle didn't seem convinced. Her dark eyes held Shanna with a mother's knowing acceptance. "I see."

Shanna wanted to fall through the floor. Gayle Adams was a shrewd woman. She'd figure this out.

But what was there to figure out? Simon was still mourning the woman he'd loved with all his heart. And Shanna had no business even thinking about the man or how he made her feel. All her life, Shanna had managed to hold out hope that one day, she'd find someone who could truly love her without conditions. Her aunt had taught her that true love was gentle and caring and sure. Shanna had seen that in her aunt and uncle's marriage. And she'd often dreamed of that for her own life. But she still held the scars of her childhood and those scars cut deep. So deep that she'd held men at arm's length for most of her adult life. Sometimes the scars outshined the hope.

This was one of those times but, oh, how she wished things could be different this time, with this man. Why would Simon change for her? And why should she bother telling him her deep, dark secrets when he probably didn't really want to hear them?

Putting Simon out of her mind, she gathered the children for their afternoon hike, making sure she put Brady and Pamela in charge of the others to give them something to do.

"I'm working, Ma."

Simon heard his mother's long-suffering sigh coming loud and clear through the air waves. "Get over here, now," she repeated. "And bring a spatula."

"A what? Never mind. I'll be there in five minutes."

He had worked. Blissfully, he'd had almost two hours of quiet. Shiloh had stayed outside and then taken off on the walk with the kids and Shanna. Let the old mutt go, Simon thought. He wanted to get his work done so *he* could...play. With Shanna.

He wanted to talk to her, and make her smile and show her she was safe with him. He'd listen to her secrets. He wouldn't judge her. But he had to also treat this much in the same way he would treat creating a pair of custom-made one-of-a-kind boots. He had to take things slow and measure precisely then he had to find the best fit and create something beautiful out of scarred rawhide. Or in this case, scarred hearts.

Grabbing a big spatula, Simon headed across the meadow to the quaint brown cabin that had always reminded him of a miniature chalet. His brother had done a good job of renovating the place into a whimsical but functional guesthouse. Funny how Simon hadn't paid much attention to that before. The little cabin was charming and inviting.

Funny how he was seeing the world with a new set of eyes today. Then he got the idea to pick some flowers to put on the picnic tables. Maybe that would make Shanna happy.

Shanna and her ragtag band of followers got back to the cabin just before sunset, the smell of hamburgers cooking on the grill causing all of them to moan with hunger.

"Dinner," Felix said, grinning over at Lavi. "I can eat at least two burgers."

Lavi made a face. "You'll throw up after you do."

"Let's just be glad we didn't have to cook," Shanna said with a smile. "But remember, we have clean-up detail."

"Why are we always having to do chores, Miss Shanna?" Marshall asked, his face squished up in a grimace. "I thought this was supposed to be a fun week."

Shanna halted on the trail then turned to face him. "Well, haven't you had fun?"

"Yes," he said. "Except for having to keep our bunks neat and always having to wash and fold clothes and carry out the trash and—"

Brady slapped at Marshall's arm. "Hey, man, that's part of the deal. We've all done stuff that got us in trouble and when you make trouble, you have to face a sentence."

Marshall pushed away. "All I did was skip school."

"Why did you do that?" Lavi asked, her straw hat covered with flowers she'd picked along the trail.

"I was bored," Marshall said. He shrugged. "Besides, I hate math and I knew I was gonna fail anyway."

"So you just gave up?" Shanna asked.

"I didn't have any choice," Marshall admitted. "Nobody at my house is good at math."

"I am," Brady said. Then he frowned and looked off into the trees.

"Would you be willing to help Marshall?" Shanna asked. She shot Brady a pleading look. "And maybe Marshall could teach you how to play the guitar. He's very good at that and I know you want to learn."

Brady looked over at Marshall. "I guess that would work. But only a couple of days after school. I work part-time at the general store. Part of *my* sentence."

Lavi kicked at a rock. "I didn't really do anything bad, Miss Shanna. But I did bop a girl for making fun of my daddy's tattoos. Then she wrote something on the wall at school. Something really bad about me. I got caught standing there arguing with her. My teacher said I wasn't supposed to fight at school or write on the wall. I didn't write on any wall, but I got in trouble anyway for that, too."

"I saw that," Pamela said. "Ugly words."

"Not nice words," Lavi replied. "I told that girl not to do it. I almost bopped her again."

"And you got in trouble for being with her?"

"Yes, ma'am. And for slapping her. Now my parents don't want me hanging out with her."

"Does she come to Youth?"

"No. She doesn't like church."

"My mom makes me come to Youth," Robert said. "But I like being out here. Can we do this again, Miss Shanna?"

Shanna looked at each of them and saw

the hope and the hesitancy in their faces. "I think we will, definitely." Then she held up a hand. "Wait up, before we go up to the cabin. I need to say something."

"Uh-oh. Are we in trouble again?" Lavi asked, her big hat down over her even bigger azure-colored eyes.

"No," Shanna replied. "We've had some moments this week, but so far you've all tried very hard to behave. And I think we have had some fun—like fishing and riding the river, eating pizza and singing songs by the campfire. Eating s'mores and grilled hotdogs. I wanted y'all to experience things this week that you normally don't get to enjoy. I wanted to let y'all know that if you ever need to talk to me, I'm always available, at school or at church, okay?"

"Okay," Lavi said, rushing to give Shanna a hug. "I love you, Miss Shanna."

The rest of the kids smiled and said pretty much the same. Shanna had to stay back to hide the tears misting in her eyes. She did love these kids and hoped they'd go back to school next week with a new attitude. She'd tried so hard to talk to them about teenage issues and anger management. Had it worked? She could only pray.

Taking a deep breath, she walked on behind them as they rounded the curve to the cabin. Then she heard Lavi gasp. "What is it?"

"Look," Lavi said, her smile impish. "It's beautiful."

Shanna glanced toward the small meadow between Simon's cabin and the rental, seeing that someone had moved the picnic tables, placing them up on the hill with the best view of the river below.

And someone had put Mason jars full of daisies, clover, red poppies, baby's breath and bachelor's buttons on each table. Old-fashioned kerosene lamps glowed from each table, illuminating the meadow in the gathering dusk of sunset. And paper lanterns lit with tiny little white lights sparkled in the low hanging branches of the trees behind the three tables. The whole place glowed.

"It is beautiful," Shanna said, letting out a gasp of her own. "Someone's been very busy."

She didn't think Gayle could have done this on her own. Simon? She didn't dare hope. Why would he go to the trouble? The man didn't even know it was spring.

Then she heard soft classical guitar music playing out over the trees. The whole scene looked like something out of a magazine display.

"C'mon, Miss Shanna."

Shanna's heart seemed to grow and expand as Lavi tugged her along, the girl's hand trusting and secure in her own. Shanna wanted to cry with joy, but beneath that sweet joy a sadness lurked and pushed.

She'd have to go back to her own world soon. And that meant she'd be leaving this secluded mountainside meadow behind. She'd be leaving Simon behind, too.

Why did that thought bring such pain?

She walked with the kids around the side of the cabin and saw Simon standing at the big barrel-shaped grill, wearing a white apron that had a grinning bear wearing a chef's hat etched on its front.

He looked adorable. And content.

Then he turned and saw her, a smile breaking across his dark features.

Shanna had to blink. Simon was smiling at her.

And he looked like he meant it.

Chapter Eleven

Simon's whole system went on alert when he looked up to find Shanna coming around the corner. Did she notice the flowers and the lanterns? Did she see the pretty tablecloths his mother had found in the big family cabin?

Did she see his smile?

She smiled back, but she didn't seem so sure.

Simon couldn't blame the woman. He'd given her so many mixed signals she probably felt like a boat lost out on the river. But tonight, things would be different. He would be nice. He could do nice.

Gayle came out the open back door, carrying the hamburgers. "All patted out for you," she said. Then she put the big pan next to the grill. "You did a great job, Simon. I'm sure Shanna will appreciate it."

Simon nodded, still unsure. "I hope so."

His mother leaned in to give him a quick peck on the cheek. "It's good to see you smiling."

Then in her typical style, his mother left it at that. For now. He knew she was probably bursting at the seams to make a match between Shanna and him, but Simon wasn't one to rush into a one-of-a-kind experience, whether it was making a pair of boots, or going back into a relationship with a woman.

He was scared silly at the very prospect.

He'd take things slow and feel his way through this. That was the only way to make something that would last a lifetime. If it was meant to last a lifetime. He still wasn't so sure what was happening here, but something had changed. His armor had been pierced.

Shanna walked up onto the deck, kids rushing around her like fireflies. "Hello."

"Hi," he said, giving her his best grin. "I'm the head cook and bottle washer tonight."

"You didn't have to bother. Everything is so lovely."

"I wanted to bother. Glad you like it."

"But I thought—"

"I want to help. It's all right."

"Is it really?" she asked, doubt dripping off the simple question. "Or did your mother force you to do all of this?"

Simon made sure they were alone. Careful to put the beef patties on the grill one at a time, he stepped back when the smoke and fire flared up. "Yes, really. Ma called me to help."

"Then you *were* forced. You don't have to feel obligated, Simon."

"Would you listen?" he said, dropping the big spatula down against the empty pan. "I admit at first, I didn't like all this commotion over here. But I've kinda gotten used to it now."

Shiloh ran up, woofed, sniffed and danced around.

Shanna reached a hand toward the big dog, automatically petting him and scratching him behind the ears. Shiloh's tongue hung out in glee.

Simon watched, his heart thumping right

along with Shiloh's tail. "This is big for me, Shanna. Big, very big. I haven't been this involved with anyone in a long time. But I'm involved with your youth group now. And it's not half bad." He wanted to tell her it could be all good, but he had to work that part out in his mind first.

She turned around to check on the kids. They were busy moving in and out, carrying paper plates and cups of ice, sodas and chips. Gayle was making sure they were all occupied.

"What'll happen next week, Simon?"

He didn't have an immediate answer for that. "What do you mean?"

"I mean, will you go back into exile? Or will you come to church so these kids can see you again?"

"And so *you* can see me again?"

She twisted away, looked out over the golden-washed water. The sun was behind them to the west, but it cast a deep, glowing sheen across the trees and the easy-flowing river. Squirrels frolicked high up in the pines. Somewhere off in the distance a dove cooed softly. "I don't know if I want to see you again."

He checked the burgers. They were beginning to crisp. Just like her new attitude. "Why not?"

Her frown was cute but full of frustration. "You can't be serious? Why not? Because you practically spelled things out to me in no uncertain terms. You're not ready for any of this. Especially not me. And besides we've only known each other for a few days. You shouldn't rush into this just because I'm the first woman you've noticed in a long time."

"Let me decide that."

"I don't want you to feel obligated—"

"You are not an obligation. You're just… confusing."

"I don't want to confuse you."

"Too late." He turned from the grill and saw the doubt surfacing with quicksilver clarity in her eyes. "I'm confused, but in a good way. I think my pulse is back."

"I'm glad to hear that," she said, bobbing her head. "But I don't want you to make promises you can't keep. You'll see once we're gone. Things will settle down and you'll realize you like your peace and quiet after all."

"I don't like being alone and lonely," he said, the words out before he could change his mind. "Not anymore."

"I don't want you to resent me," she said on a small whisper. "Just remember that."

Then she turned to go and help his mother.

Leaving Simon to think his grand gesture hadn't made things any better after all.

"You didn't eat very much."

Gayle pointed to Shanna's plate. Her burger was half gone, her chips dried out now. And her slice of strawberry pie from the three that Jolena had sent was missing only a bite or two.

"I'm working on it," Shanna said, her elbows propped up on the table while she watched the kids and Simon play a lively game of volleyball. "Guess I wasn't as hungry as I thought."

"He's trying, you know."

Shanna gave Gayle a sideways stare. "Simon, you mean?"

"Who else? A mother worries about her children. And since my husband died, I've had double duty on that, let me tell you."

Her smile was bittersweet, a small twist of her lips. "Rick's settled now and happy, but I have to admit I had my doubts about Cari when she first came back to town."

"But now?"

"Now, I can see how much she loves my son. So I don't have to worry anymore about him. But Simon? I've always worried about him. He was quiet growing up, a real loner. Then he found Marcy wearing a pair of boots and that gave him his passion for his work. She brought out the quiet artist inside my son. She was such a joy. Always cooking and laughing, always singing and making funny little jokes."

Shanna swallowed the tightness in her throat cutting off her breath. "Her death was hard on all of you, I imagine."

"Very hard. She died, then my husband died, too. I thought my heart would never recover."

"I'm sorry," Shanna said, putting her hand over Gayle's. "It must have been awful." She pushed her own dark thoughts away. Her aunt always told Shanna she'd have to deal with her own grief one day, but she didn't know how. If she opened that floodgate, she might never recover.

"It was tough," Gayle said, patting her hand. "But with the grace of God and my church family, I managed to get past the worst of it. Now I just want my boys to be happy. Every mother wants that for her children."

"Not every mother," Shanna said, grief and regret cutting at her heart.

"What do you mean?"

She looked out toward the meadow to the spot where the grass was clear and green, the spot where Simon had set up an old volleyball net so they could play. "My mother didn't care if I was happy or not."

"Tell me about her," Gayle said, her hand still on Shanna's.

Shanna swallowed, wondered if she dared to speak. "She died when I was around thirteen, and I went to live with Aunt Claire and Uncle Doug."

"Oh, honey, I'm so sorry. Is that why your aunt and uncle raised you?"

Shanna nodded, wishing she could close the door on the horrible memories. "Yes. I didn't have anyone else."

"What happened?"

Shanna couldn't say the words. She'd tried to run from the truth and she wasn't ready to divulge that truth yet, not here, not now.

"It's a long story. I'd rather not get into it with the kids around."

"I understand," Gayle said, getting up to gather paper plates. "I didn't mean to intrude."

"It's not that," Shanna said. "It's just I don't want to get upset in front of them."

"Okay." Gayle dumped the paper plates into the trash. "If you ever need to talk—"

"I know I can trust you," Shanna said, smiling. "I appreciate you, Miss Gayle."

"And I appreciate you," Gayle replied. "You've managed to bring my son out of his shell."

"For now," Shanna said, watching as Simon spiked the ball then high-fived Brady.

Gayle tidied up the table then brushed her hands down her jeans. "I think for good."

Two hours later, the kids were all settled down with a movie and Katie was asleep in the room she was sharing with Shanna. Gayle had walked across to her own cabin to spend the night. Shanna was restless, the animated movie's action-packed pace making her more so.

"I'm going out on the deck for a while," she told Pamela. "Watch out for Katie, okay?"

Pamela nodded. Since the episode earlier in the day when she and Brady had sneaked away, the girl had been quiet but on her best behavior. Shanna wondered if Pamela and Brady were just biding their time until they were back in school. She worried about what might happen between the two.

And prayed they'd make the right choices, no matter how they felt about each other.

Now if she could only do the same in her life.

Things had been going so well since she'd moved to Knotwood Mountain last fall. Cari and Rick had been supportive and helpful, and Shanna had made a lot of good friends at school and at church. She felt as if she'd finally found a place of her own, the kind of hometown she'd always dreamed about. The kind of place her mother used to tell her about.

Shanna missed those rare quiet moments she'd had with her mother, before things had turned so ugly. Before her life had turned into a tragedy.

"One day, Shanna. One day, we'll find the perfect little town to live in and you'll be a hometown sweetheart. Everybody will know you and love you. And all of this will be a distant memory."

Her mother had been making up fairy tales. Shanna had learned she couldn't rely on such promises. But coming here to the quiet beauty of Knotwood Mountain had given her a fresh start.

Now, she wondered if she'd made the right decision. Now that Simon had stepped bigger than life right into her world, she had to wonder if she'd wind up being hurt yet again. Or worse, if she'd hurt him.

Sooner or later, someone would find out the sordid details of her past and then what? Would people shun her, turn away from her, judge her? Pity her?

How would Simon feel about her if he knew?

That thought only made her even more unsettled and restless. She prayed for peace, for answers.

Then she saw a light shining in Simon's workshop and before she knew it, she was standing at the open screen door, watching as he quietly went about his work.

Fascinated, Shanna glanced back toward her cabin. She couldn't leave the kids alone for very long. Something might happen. Anything could happen.

But for just a few precious minutes, she enjoyed seeing the soft sheen of concentration on Simon's face. He truly did come alive when he was working. His talent was evident, his dedication admirable. But had he used his work as a shield to hide all of his pain? Had God called Simon to use his talent?

Was she doing the same, pouring all of her energy into saving children, one at a time? But hadn't God called her to do that?

Or were they both shielding themselves from any type of close relationships, maybe living vicariously through their work and actions, rather than their own hearts and emotions?

She turned to go, her mind in turmoil, but a sound inside stopped her.

"Shanna?"

Why had she come over here? Why had she disturbed him yet again? Shanna started down the steps.

"Hey, come back."

He was out the door in two seconds flat, his hand catching at her cotton shirt. "Is everything okay?" He glanced toward her cabin then back to her. "What's wrong?"

"I came out for some air. The kids are watching a movie. I need to get back."

"I'll walk with you, then."

Shiloh showed up at the door. "Go on back," Simon said, causing the dog to woof a protest. "I need to let him out before we go to bed."

Shanna nodded, unable to speak. Simon opened the door then called to the dog. Shiloh bounded out and nudged Shanna, then ran off into the woods.

Simon took her hand in his. Shiloh barked

softly at some unseen animal rustling around near the river.

"Okay, talk to me. What's the matter?"

"I didn't mean to interrupt you," she managed to get out. "I was just feeling a little blue."

"You, blue?" He smiled, his finger touching on her chin. "You're the original Susie Sunshine, aren't you?"

She pulled away. "No, I'm not and maybe that's the problem. I've built a nice facade for the world, Simon. But I haven't been honest with you. And I think maybe it's time for me to tell you the truth. I can't let you go on believing I have all the answers, that I'm some sort of Pollyanna who's always happy. It's not fair. It's not right."

He stood still, his frown silhouetted in moonlight. "You're not making any sense, Shanna."

"None of it makes any sense," she said, wishing she could let go and trust that God would see her through.

Simon surprised her then. He pulled her into his arms and whispered into her ear. "I'm here. I'm not going anywhere. And I've been wrong to assume that I'm the only one who's ever been through trauma and grief. Talk to me, Shanna. Help me to understand."

How could she explain something she couldn't even understand herself?

"It's a long story."

"Let's go sit on your porch so we can listen for the kids."

They made it to the steps when the back door burst open and Brady and Marshall fell out and rolled onto the deck, fists flying in the air as they tried to beat each other to a pulp.

Chapter Twelve

"Hey!" Simon hurled himself between the two kids, grabbing each one by the collar. "Enough."

Brady yanked away, his face burning with anger. "He started it."

Marshall rolled to his feet, blood flowing from his nose. "Did not. You did."

Shanna held up a hand. "Okay, Brady, what happened?"

Brady tried to catch his breath, his chest rising and falling as he glared over at Marshall. "He was messing with Pammie. I told him to lay off."

Felix and Robert showed up, both talking at once. "That's the truth, Miss Shanna," Robert said. "We all heard Marshall picking on her. We told him to shut up so we could watch the movie."

Pamela came out onto the porch with Lavi. The two girls clung to each other. Pamela sniffed back tears. "I think I want to go home, Miss Shanna. I can't deal with this anymore."

Brady looked crushed, then shrugged. "Whatever. I was just trying to protect you. Look where that got me."

The girl started crying again. "You get so mad all the time, Brady. It scares me."

Shanna's heart hammered and knocked. How many times had she heard that when she was young, over and over. Her mother telling her stepfather that he scared her. He'd scared both of them. But her mother always forgave him. Always.

"Why did Brady get mad?" Simon asked, his hands on his hips. "And I want the truth."

Marshall pushed at his bushy hair. "I called Pammie a name and he didn't like it."

"And what did you call her?" Simon stepped closer. "You'd better tell me, right now."

Brady held up a fist. "Tell him or I'll hit you again."

Marshall whispered a derogatory phrase.

Pammie started crying again and Brady took a step, his fists curled at his side.

"Don't ever call her that again," he said on a low growl. "I mean it, Marshall. You're always calling people names and making fun of them. Then you have to play all your silly jokes. That's what got you in trouble at school, remember?"

Marshall held up his hands then dropped them at his side. "Why am I always the one who gets blamed? I've heard you say worse, Brady."

"Not anymore," Brady said, lifting his chin. "I try not to, not anymore."

"Well, good for you," Marshall retorted on a smirk. "So, you're better than the rest of us now that you're such a fine church-goer? Now that you hang with that do-gooder Cari?"

"I didn't say that," Brady replied. "It's not that easy."

"Not, it's not," Simon said, giving Shanna a reassuring glance. "Shanna, why don't you take the other boys and girls back inside. I'd like to talk to these two privately."

"Are you sure?" She didn't want Simon to do her job.

If *she'd* been doing her job, this wouldn't have happened. She knew not to leave the kids alone, not for one second. This incident and the one with Brady and Pamela earlier were both good reasons to put Simon and the way he made her feel out of her mind for good. She had a responsibility to these children and that came ahead of everything else. Especially her attraction to Simon.

"Let me talk to them," he said, his expression changing from annoyed to calm. "Man-to-man."

She almost told him no, but she was too upset to take on the task herself. She might say something she'd regret. Normally, she could have handled this but being around Simon caused her to make bad decisions. Leaving the kids alone was one of those. And this fight only reminded her of all the horrible things she'd tried so hard to fight against.

"C'mon, let's give them some space," she said to the others. "It's getting late anyway. Time for bed."

"We didn't get to finish watching the movie," Robert said. "That is so not fair."

Shanna could have told him a lot of

things weren't fair. And sometimes things didn't turn out for the best, no matter how hard you tried to make them work. Maybe this week was one of those things.

Simon guided the two huffing teens to one of the picnic tables. "Sit," he said, motioning to the table top.

Brady slipped up onto the table, daring Marshall with a heated frown to get near him. Marshall slinked against the far side of the wooden table, his long arms wrapped around his stomach, blood congealed below his nose.

Simon took a deep breath. "You know something? I didn't realize until now how blessed I am to have this place. It's a nice, quiet bit of acreage. Far away from the tourists and the crowded restaurants. Not much happens out here. I like that. I *liked* that. But I have to say, this week has opened my eyes to a lot of things."

"You hate us," Brady said, lifting his head. "Just say it. We're the troublemakers, the bad kids. Except Pammie's not really so bad. She…she just skips school sometimes, to get away from everything."

"I used to skip school," Simon replied, trying to find some common ground. "Until my daddy found out. I had to do all my brother's chores plus mine for three long months. And I didn't get to go to summer camp. Had to sweep floors in the general store." He held his hands up high then dropped his arms to his side. "And look at me now. On top of the world."

Or at least he had been.

"So you do hate us," Brady retorted, reminding Simon that he still had some attitude left.

"I don't hate anybody. I kinda like all of you. And I know I'm old and not so cool, but I've been where you are right now. My brother and I used to fight right over there on our porch. One time, we broke the porch rail and had to spend the next weekend fixing it instead of being out with our girls. My daddy made sure we'd better have a very good reason to pull punches the next time, let me tell you."

"Why did y'all fight?" Marshall asked, shooting a glare toward Brady.

"Why? Because we're brothers and we're both stubborn. Still are. We don't fight like that anymore, but we have some heated discussions."

"But you love each other," Marshall replied, his tone softening. "That can't be all bad."

"It's not all bad," Simon replied, seeing his life in a different light. "We've been blessed. Our father was a good man, but a strict man. Our mother loves us and tries to take care of us even now. So, yes, we love each other." He kicked at the table legs. "So why can't y'all just get along while you're here? Shanna went to a lot of trouble to make this week fun and interesting. She wants y'all to see that life can be good even when you're confused and mixed up and…a teenager."

Brady put his hands together over his knees and stared down at the ground. "He shouldn't have called Pammie that name."

"No, he shouldn't have." Simon glanced over at Marshall. "Why do you call people names, anyway, Marshall?"

Marshall shrugged. "Dunno. My daddy has a name for everybody, even me and my brother and sister, when he's mad at us. Guess I heard it from him. He hates his job, talks bad about his boss and takes it out on us. Then he laughs about it."

"And you think that's the right way to handle things?"

"I dunno," Marshall said, getting up. "I'm sorry I called Pammie that. I didn't mean it. It was a joke."

"It might be a joke to you," Simon told the boy, "but it hurts the people who are the butt of that joke."

He finally sat down on the other table across from them. "Look, I'm not here to lecture or to pass judgment. I'm certainly not the best authority on this. But I can tell you right now, that men need to respect women. Brady, we talked about this earlier when you went off with Pammie. It's all about respect, boys. Respect for each other, for girls and for yourselves, get it?"

"Yes, sir." Brady glanced over at Marshall. "Just don't do that again, man."

Marshall tipped his chin up. "Okay. I said I was sorry. Can I go to bed now?"

Simon felt helpless. Had he even made a dent in their thick skulls? Would they fight again, or do something worse, once they were back in school? He hoped not. That kind of behavior would destroy Shanna.

Shanna. She'd been on the verge of telling him something. He's seen it there in her eyes. The pain, the hurt, the dread. He didn't want to see that look in her eyes ever again. And he wasn't so sure he wanted to hear what she had to say. Not that he wasn't interested or that he didn't care. He did. Maybe too much.

He just wasn't sure he could handle anything that had caused that haunted look in her pretty eyes.

But would she put the walls back up now? Would she hide behind that sunny smile and cheerful disposition and never open up to him? Simon might be the one hiding out in the woods, but Shanna seemed to be the one hiding behind a brave façade. She'd told him as much earlier.

He got up and held out his hand to Brady. "Okay, I've said enough. I don't have all the answers. Just try to be kind to each other. And show respect for the girls and for Miss Shanna." He shook Brady's hand then turned to Marshall and reached out to him. "Understand?"

Marshall reluctantly shook his hand then got up and stalked away. Brady stared after him. "His old man beats him," he said, his voice low. "His daddy isn't very nice."

"All the more reason for *you* to try and be nice," Simon replied, appalled by some of the things he'd heard and seen this week. "But, Brady, I'm impressed that you stood up for Pammie."

"She hates me now, though."

"Anger scares people. You scared her tonight. Apologize and try to do better."

"My mom makes me go to a therapist since that thing with vandalizing Cari's house and all."

"That's good," Simon replied, remembering the aching grief he'd suffered after Marcy died. "I had to do that same thing when my wife passed away. I was angry at everyone, including God."

Brady gave him a long stare. "I don't know why I get so mad. It just comes over me."

Simon certainly understood that feeling.

"Self-control is hard, but you might try counting to ten or telling yourself it's just not worth losing your temper over the little stuff. I don't know. I'm sure your therapist will help with that."

Brady got up and brushed off his shorts. "I just want Pammie to be okay. I really like her."

Simon walked with him toward the cabin. "Tomorrow is a new day. You can show her how sorry you are. Pick her some flowers or something." Like that had worked for him, Simon thought, his own heart morose.

"What if she goes home early?"

"Then you'll survive. I promise you will."

Brady's face crinkled in a tight smile. "I guess so. I don't get girls sometimes, anyway."

"Neither do I, buddy," Simon said. "Neither do I."

He watched Brady go inside then turned back toward his own cabin. He wouldn't push Shanna. She'd talk to him when she felt comfortable with him. But he wanted to know everything there was to know about her, because he couldn't stand the thought of her being sad or scared or unsure.

He couldn't take that. Because he cared about her. Just like Brady felt about Pammie, Simon really liked Shanna.

And if they all get through this week, he aimed to continue liking her. And flirting with her. And maybe taking her out to dinner now and then. He hadn't been out to dinner with a pretty woman since...

Since Marcy.

Did he dare take the next step with Shanna?

It was a start. A scary, unstable, confusing, amazing, remarkable, unpredictable start.

And maybe it was about time he started over anyway.

But only if Shanna was ready, too.

Chapter Thirteen

Shanna heard a car coming up the long drive to the cabin then glanced up to see Cari's smiling face behind the wheel of Rick's Jeep.

Glad to see her best friend, she also went into panic mode. Had something happened to Katie's grandmother? Shanna had talked to Janie last night and given Janie a good report on Katie's day. Surely Cari would have called if something bad had happened. And she wouldn't be smiling.

"I need to think positive," Shanna mumbled to herself. Even if the week had gone from bad to worse at times, she had to believe she'd done the right thing, bringing the kids out to the river for this retreat.

Cari got out, dressed in khaki shorts and hiking shoes, her tote bag revealing a bright pink and green beach towel. "Good morning."

"Hi," Shanna said, getting up from the picnic table where they'd had breakfast and their morning devotional. "What are you doing here?"

Cari looked around and waved at the kids going to and fro, cleaning up their breakfast dishes. "I had the day off and decided to come and help you."

"How'd you get a day off in the middle of the week?"

Cari laughed and sat down next to Shanna. "Jolena's oldest daughter helps me out in the shop a lot. She's so good with the customers I can afford to leave her to it every now and then. She has Rick next door and her mother across the way at the diner, so she'll be fine. She wants to open her own shop one day. And she's learning how to design jewelry, too."

Shanna nodded at that. "You're a great teacher and artist."

"Yes, I am," Cari replied with a smug

grin, her green eyes sparkling. "Which is why I brought my supplies today. I thought maybe the kids might want to make some trinkets." She held up a hand. "I brought manly stuff, too. Leather strips and grainy dark stones—for the boys."

"Good thinking." Shanna said. "And it's nice to see a friendly face."

Cari elbowed her. "Yeah, Gayle told me you've had some ups and downs. I warned you about taking on this group."

Shanna let out a sigh then looked over to Simon's workshop. "You did warn me about the cranky neighbor, too. But I've managed to hold my own with all of them."

"Gayle also mentioned that. Seems you've managed to bring Simon out of hiding?"

"Not really." Shanna wasn't even sure she could talk to Cari about the man. "He's been a big help, but reluctantly. We keep disturbing him. I'm not sure he likes having us next door. I'll have to find another cabin next year, I think."

Cari leaned back, her honey-colored curls shimmering in the morning sunshine. "If Simon's been hanging around, trust me, he likes it. Or more to the point, he likes you. We've all tried to get him out of seclusion. When I first met him, I was sure he hated me."

"Yeah, I got that same feeling," Shanna replied, the memory of his kisses and his kindness toward her and the kids making her smile. "He's more bark than bite, you know."

"I do know," Cari replied. "So where is he now?"

"I'm not sure. Probably catching up on work. He's dedicated to his craft and he's behind schedule because of fooling around with us. I admire that about him—the way he works so hard."

"Takes one to know one. You're dedicated to your work, too. Not many people would want to spend spring break with a bunch of unruly teens, especially after teaching high schoolers all year."

"I wanted to make a difference with them. And I love having Katie here."

"How's she doing?"

Shanna could at least rest assured on that issue. "She's blossoming. The older kids have been surprisingly careful with her.

They make sure she's always safe and taken care of, they pamper her and play games with her. Pammie and Lavi have both been a great help to her." She motioned toward Simon's workshop. "She even won over Grumpy."

Cari laughed at that. "I know you were worried about bringing her, since she's so young."

"Yes, but having her grandmother helped, until Janie got sick. I talked to her last night before I went to bed. Her indigestion is much better but Lee won't let her come back out here. Do you think there's something else wrong with her, something she'd not telling us?"

"I think Lee's just being protective," Cari said, sitting up straight, concern in her eyes. "I haven't heard anything through the Knotwood Mountain grapevine. And if Miss Janie is really bad-off sick, it would be all over this mountain."

Relief washed over Shanna, dark memories swirling around her like glistening currents. "Good. I'm glad. That little girl needs her grandparents."

Cari sat silent for a while then asked, "Have you talked to your aunt this week?"

Shanna interpreted that to mean "How are you doing?" Cari knew Shanna worried about her aging aunt and uncle. If anything happened to them, she'd be all alone. Again.

"I've managed to call her between nature walks and making s'mores, yes. She's great. They're both great. They're planning a visit here later in the summer."

"Glad to hear it."

The kids came back toward the tables, laughing and talking. Cari leaned close. "Have you told Simon anything about yourself?"

"Not all of it," Shanna said on a taut whisper. "And I think I'll keep it that way for now."

She was glad they'd been interrupted by the fight last night, for more reasons than she could ever explain. What if she had spilled her guts to Simon? Would he have listened politely then turned to go home? Would he have stared at her as if she had an incurable disease, the way some men had in the past when she'd opened up to them?

Somehow, the thought of Simon turning away from her made her wish for things she couldn't explain. Of the few men she'd dated or gotten to know, his opinion was the most important one. She couldn't bear the pity, the disgust she'd probably see in his eyes. And she didn't want pity to be a catalyst for any deeper feelings between them.

Maybe if she remained a friend to him and nothing more, she wouldn't have to delve too much into her childhood miseries. Maybe.

"Cari!" Brady rushed up, giving Cari a high five. "I was washing dishes but Felix told me you were here. What're you doing here?"

Shanna put thoughts of Simon away for now. Her first priority was to this youth group. She needed to remember that.

"Came to hang out with y'all all day," Cari said. "Thought I'd catch some rays, maybe swim in Rick's favorite spot where the river runs into a little creek. Then we can make some jewelry. That is, if it's okay with your schedule."

Shanna nodded. "We'd planned to sun

and swim today anyway. Or did you already know that, too?"

"Yeah. Gayle mentioned it." Cari grinned. "I couldn't miss out on showing the kids the secret swimming hole. Rick and his brother used to play on the tire swing back there all summer long, according to the tales they tell."

Brady grunted. "Simon said they used to fight and get in trouble. He had to do all of Rick's chores one summer."

"I don't doubt that," Cari said, grinning. "Boys will be boys."

Shanna could picture Rick and Simon going head to head. She breathed a sigh of relief, seeing the mirth in Brady's eyes. Maybe Simon's presence had helped the kid after all. And maybe Simon had done something she wasn't able to do—open up and really talk about his past. Or the good parts of his past.

Wondering if she'd see him today, Shanna told herself to get back into the here and now. Seeing Simon shouldn't be on her agenda. She had kids to take care of and entertain.

"Well, let's gather our stuff and head

out," she said, glad Cari had come to help out. "It looks like another pretty day." At least the weather had cooperated all week even if the local forecast was predicting rain for later today and over the weekend.

Cari nudged her. "Hey, want me to go get Simon? He'll be jealous of us taking over his favorite swimming spot."

"No, I do not. You know, your family needs to stop trying to push us together. The man's nice to look at and somewhat pleasant to be around, but he's only *being* nice until I'm out of his hair. I'm not so desperate that I'd force a man to spend time with me."

"Nobody forces Simon," Cari countered. "I'm telling you, I saw sparks between you two the other night at the Pizza Haus."

"You're imagining things." But Shanna had to admit, *she* felt sparks each time the man came around. Especially when he leaned close and kissed her. And because she didn't want to seem petty, she said, "I'd like to be his friend. I think he could use a good friend."

"That works," Cari said. "Friendship can often lead to something else."

"Not this time." But Shanna couldn't deny the little thread of hope dangling inside her heart like that rope swing Cari had mentioned.

Simon noticed it right away. He lifted his head. Then Shiloh did the same, probably thinking his master knew something he didn't.

Silence.

Simon eyed the open windows and listened again.

Shiloh whimpered and stood up to nudge Simon's knee.

"Quit fretting," Simon said to the big dog. "So you weren't invited to play with your friends today. Better rest up, you old mutt. Use this time wisely, I say."

While he used this time to work. But the silence was making him restless. And when had that changed? A week ago, he'd relished the silence, treasured the isolation, needed the peace and quiet.

A week ago, he hadn't known Shanna.

So he sat staring at the starlet's boots he'd just finished, his calloused hands touching on the smooth, shiny leather.

The boots started out a deep rich brown trimmed in a vanilla cream at the seams. Those colors met up with the vivid yellow lightning flashes covering the brown boots. He wanted to be done with this order so he could get back to work on Shanna's boots.

"Not bad," Simon said, deciding that in spite of all the interruptions and distractions, these boots had turned out pretty good. He knew the starlet would like them. And he also knew the minute she wore them to some big event, he'd start getting calls for more orders. That's how his life went. He worked and worked and then he waited for more orders to fill the void. He didn't like the void.

Thankfully, over the last five or so years he'd been busy enough to keep his mind off other things. When Marcy was alive and they were happy, he'd worked on his boot orders and also worked the land around the cabins and sometimes went into town to help out at the store.

Then she'd gotten sick and he'd given up everything else but making a pair of boots now and then. He had spent most of his time by her side, either at the doctor's office in Atlanta, or at Emory Hospital in the cancer center, sitting by her bed.

Simon held one of the boots up, his gaze scanning the outsole, the heel breast, the light brown wingtips, remembering the days he'd escape out here for a couple of hours, his heart breaking in half, while his mother or a neighbor sat with Marcy. Sometimes, her parents would take over, maybe sensing his pain, to allow him some rest and time alone.

He'd always craved time alone to think, to pray, to ponder life. He liked to read by a lamp in a silent house or with one of his favorite country artists playing in the background. He had no need for too much television or too much noise. He was content until the awful day when he'd found out his wife was sick.

And after Marcy had died, he'd often sit, just sit, staring out the big window, the sound of the river moving down the mountain like a lullaby trying to soothe his soul. He'd hear the birds chirping and fussing in the big live oak out in the meadow. He'd see a deer strolling gracefully and quietly along, or watch for butterflies moving through the wildflowers. Marcy loved butterflies.

She'd died in winter. A cold, dark, misty winter.

Simon hated winter.

He dropped the boot. Now all of that had changed. Like the river currents, his meandering soul had shifted and moved and formed a new path. But he was drowning.

"I think I'm in over my head, Lord."

Staring at her unfinished boots sitting on a nearby shelf, he wondered where Shanna was this morning. Then he heard a door slam and he was up and out of his chair. Simon didn't like spying, but he wanted to see her.

When he saw Brady with the first-aid kit, his heart hit hard against his chest and he headed out with Shiloh, careful to lock things up before he left. What had Snow White and the Seven Troublemakers gotten into this time?

Chapter Fourteen

"Poison ivy."

Shanna watched as Felix and Marshall both scratched at their legs. "I can't believe we got into poison ivy."

"Not all of us," Cari replied, slapping at her own legs in mock concern. "Katie doesn't seem to be itching, thankfully."

"I think it's just me and Marshall," Felix said, hopping on one foot. "Man, it sure does itch."

"Brady should be here soon with the first-aid kit," Shanna replied. "I brought sunscreen and bug spray but I never considered this."

Cari checked Pammie and Lavi. "Are you two itching?"

They both shook their heads. "We didn't

go as far down into the creek as they did," Lavi said. "They went through those bushes over there." She pointed to an outcropping of overgrown shrubs and vines. "They went in there first thing when we got here this morning."

"I told them a snake might be in there," Robert said before plowing back into the water.

Felix and Marshall went toward the shallow eddies, both scratching at their stomach and legs. Shanna could hear their mumblings from where she sat on a rock over the water. "I don't know what could possibly go wrong next."

Then she heard a dog barking.

Cari shot her a bemused look. "I think Grumpy has come a'calling."

"Great, just what I needed." Shanna got up and tossed her T-shirt over her wet one-piece and cut-off shorts.

Shiloh came rushing through the foliage, his happy grin a contrast to the frown on Simon's face. "Everything okay?" he asked, Brady right behind him.

"We're fine," Shanna replied, irritated that the man obviously thought she was an accident waiting to happen. "Just a little patch of poison ivy. I sent Brady to get the first-aid kit. I think there's some lotion in there."

Simon looked down at where Felix and Marshall stood in the water. "That won't help, boys. I've got some tea tree oil here. Brady told me what happened, so I went back and got it." He held up a bottle of yellow liquid and a small glass bottle of amber liquid. "I'd wash it with dishwashing detergent first then put some of this oil on it."

Cari shot Shanna another amused look. "The man is full of surprises."

"You can say that again," Shanna said on a low breath. "Amazing."

"Well, he is the original mountain man."

"Yep. Grumpy and Scruffy."

Cari chuckled then looked up to find Simon staring at them. "Sorry, I'm impressed with your knowledge about remedies for poison ivy," she said.

"I learned it firsthand, right here in these woods," he retorted, his gaze fixating on Shanna. "And who told y'all you could come to our secret watering hole anyway?"

"Your mother," they both said in unison.

"Traitor," he replied, but he smiled when he said it. "I guess this place could use some fresh swimmers. Rick and I rarely get to come back here anymore."

"C'mon in," Robert said. "The water's just right."

Simon looked longingly at the clear, shallow water. "Nah. Can't. Just wanted to make sure everyone was okay. Katie, you didn't get in those vines, did you?"

"No, sir," Katie said, giggling. "I've been chasing minnows."

"Good luck with that," Simon replied. "They're slippery."

Shanna could say the same about some men, but she kept silent, taking in the essence of his male stance and his mysterious eyes. What did he really think about all of this? About her?

A rumble off in the distance brought their staring contest to an end. "Looks like that rain might be coming in early," he said, turning to the west. "Sky's getting dark behind those trees."

"What an old fussy pants," Cari said

under her breath. "Does he always hover this way?"

Shanna lowered her head, hoping the rain wouldn't turn into a storm. "When he's around, yes."

"Ah, that's sweet. He wants to take care of you."

"He wants us gone."

She looked up to find Simon standing right in front her again. "I'm right here, you know."

"We know," Cari said, getting up to poke him in the ribs. "You're like the camp guard or something."

"Me? I came down here with Brady to see if y'all were okay."

"To check on Shanna," Cari retorted.

"No, well, yes. I mean, I don't know. I was concerned."

"Thank you," Shanna said, getting up to rescue him from Cari's unrelenting teasing. "I appreciate it."

She turned to where Felix and Marshall stood rubbing dishwashing detergent all over their legs. "We need to go. Y'all can wash that off with the outside spigot and then put the tree tea oil on back at the cabin. We don't want detergent in the river."

"Would it hurt my minnows?" Katie asked, her long hair dripping with water.

"It might," Shanna replied. "We like to leave the land and the water the way we found it."

Another rumble of thunder jarred the air, followed by a lightning strike. "Okay, let's get out of here," Shanna called, her heart rumbling right along with the thunder. "Rain's coming in." She did not like storms. Not at all.

"Well, it started out to be a pretty day," Cari said, gathering wet towels and potato chip bags. "Make sure you get all your trash. I brought a trash bag." Then she grinned. "Hey, now we can make jewelry."

The girls cheered while the boys made faces.

The kids brought their empty soda cans and cracker wrappers. Soon the whole place was clean, but the sky was growing darker by the minute. The clouds turned smoky gray.

"Did the weather man mention how bad this might be?" Shanna asked Simon. "I didn't turn on the television this morning but the boys told me it might rain."

"I think he said something about a possible late afternoon thunderstorm and storms later. I didn't expect it so soon."

"Well, I guess it's a good thing you came down to check on us."

His frown softened. "You would have heard the thunder."

Shanna forced lightness into her words. "Yes, I'm sure I would have. But thanks, anyway, for the detergent and the tea tree oil. I'm sure the boys will appreciate it."

His face twisted, not quite a smile, not quite a frown. "I hope so. It works for me. If they keep itching you might wanna find another solution. That cream in your kit might help for a little while. Or they can get shots."

Shanna nodded, eyeing the darkening skies. "Two days left. I have to admit I'm tired. I've had fun, but I'm tired." She hadn't been sleeping very well, thanks to him.

He helped her carry supplies up the hill toward the path back to the cabin. Shanna noticed Cari had corralled the others back to a safe distance. Was her friend giving her time alone with Simon?

If so, Simon didn't seem to notice. "You've had an interesting week here. Think you'll ever do it again?"

"I haven't decided," she replied, trying to keep things on an even keel. "If I do, I might try another location."

"Why?"

She had to smile at the surprise in his dark eyes.

"Uh, so we won't pester you."

"You haven't exactly pestered me. You're kinda growing on me."

"Does that mean you'll miss us when we're gone?"

He stopped on the path, his eyes capturing hers, a rich darkness swirling in his gaze. "I'll miss *you*."

Then he took off again, leaving her to catch her breath and follow, the sheer joy of that look he'd given her making it hard to move. It was the first time he'd even hinted at something more between them.

And it scared her almost as much as that booming thunder erupting in the sky.

* * *

The rain hit about halfway up the path. The kids who'd been splashing in the water just minutes before were now complaining that they were cold and wet.

Katie ran by, shivering. Shanna was shivering, too.

Simon grabbed a towel out of her big tote. "Here. Put this over your shoulders."

"Thanks. We'll be home soon," she said, still shivering. But maybe it wasn't from the rain. Maybe she was still unsure about him.

Taking her bright blue tote, Simon threw it over his arm so he could continue carrying the ice chest. Did they bring the whole kitchen with them? Then he called to Katie, "C'mere, sweetie. Stick by me."

Katie did that, her hand reaching for Simon's with such trust it floored him. Already, he cared about little Katie. What would it be like to have a child of his own? Could he survive the worries, the fears of being a parent?

The wind picked up and the light rain turned into a heavy downpour. "Go," he shouted over the wind. "I've got Katie."

Shanna and Cari ran ahead, the rest of the kids following, and Katie squealing as Simon lifted her up and held her close while he carried the ice chest by its handle with his other hand. Simon managed to get the ice chest up onto the deck. Then he handed Katie off to Brady.

"Come inside," Shanna called from under the elves. "Wait here until the rain stops."

Shiloh rushed to the door. Simon decided that for once, he agreed with the dog. No point in running through the storm. Besides, he didn't want to go home right now.

Cari was already getting things organized. "Wet towels and bathing suits in the hallway by the washing machine. Get dried off and dressed. We'll get creative for a while with my trinkets. Then we'll figure out supper."

Simon stood at the door, dripping. Shanna hurried over to hand him a dry towel. "Thanks for helping. Seems I'm always saying that to you."

Simon wanted to say so many things but his throat closed up and he couldn't seem to move his lips. That moment out there by the pond when he'd looked straight into her pretty eyes—that moment had unnerved him and left him so unsettled he wasn't sure what to say or do next.

"I don't mind helping you. I'm always trying to convince *you* of that."

"I know," she finally said, a towel in her hands. "We'll be gone in two days. I don't want—"

"Miss Shanna, I'm starving. What are we gonna eat?"

She turned, dropped her towel on the table and put her hands on her hips. Cute as a button, she hollered over the whines and questions. "You just had chips and dip and cookies. Give me a minute to get out of these wet clothes."

Simon watched as she stomped toward her room and then he went to Cari. "I can make chili."

"What?" Cari looked as flabbergasted as a squirrel running into a hawk.

"I said, I can make chili. Let me go change. I have meat and spices. I'll need tomato sauce and whatever else you can find to throw in there."

Snapping out of her stupor, Cari opened cabinets. "We have tomato paste left from the spaghetti the other night. And some spices, too. I think we have peppers and onions in the crisper. Are you sure?"

"Yes, I'm sure," he said, throwing up his hands. "Why does everyone ask me that?"

Cari lifted an eyebrow. "Maybe because you usually run the other way whenever anyone shows up around here."

"I'm changing," he said, turning to head out the door. "In case you haven't noticed."

Cari shot him a broad grin. "Really now? Are you sure?"

"You're not funny," he called out as he ran over to his place and got wet all over again. He'd bring an umbrella when he came back.

Shanna came out of her room to the sight of a big pot bubbling on the stove and the spicy smell of chili in the air. "Cari, are you cooking?"

"Me, mercy no," Cari replied, looking up from where she sat at the table surrounded by girls making necklaces and bracelets. "Simon's making chili."

Shanna came around the counter and saw him standing there all fresh and dry in jeans and a navy T-shirt. "Did you say Simon is cooking?"

"Yes, I'm cooking." Simon looked affronted. "I can cook."

Cari sent Shanna a warning look. "Grumpy's in the kitchen."

"And stop calling me that. Didn't we talk to the kids about name-calling?"

"He's right," Shanna said, wondering how they'd managed to settle down the kids. "They'll pick up on it and tease him."

Cari giggled. "If the name fits—"

"Cari!"

"Okay, okay. I'll leave you alone since that chili smells so good. Can I call Rick to come and eat with us?"

Simon rolled his eyes. "You're staying?"

"Wouldn't miss this for the world," Cari replied. She walked away with her cell phone, not waiting for his consent.

Shanna saw the affectionate way Cari and Simon sparred like a true brother and sister. Why couldn't she feel that comfortable around the man? If she wanted to be his friend, she needed to lighten up.

Glancing outside, she prayed the worst of the bad weather was over.

"That does smell good," she said, making an effort. "Where are the boys?"

He glanced over his shoulder toward the hallway. "Felix and Marshall are in their room, probably using up that whole bottle of tea tree oil. Brady wanted to take a nap. Pammie and Lavi have painted their toenails and Katie's and now they're making fashionable baubles, as you can see. And I think Robert's in the shower, washing off the mud."

"Wow."

"What's that supposed to mean?"

"Just wow," Shanna said, glancing over at the busy girls. "Thanks."

"Don't thank me again."

"I'm sorry."

"And don't apologize again." He whirled around so fast, he bumped into her.

Shanna caught her breath, tried to focus. He reached up, his hands grapping her arms, his gaze centered on her with a whipstitch accuracy. "You need to understand something. I don't do this kind of thing."

"I know."

"No, you don't know. And I'm not explaining myself very well. I don't do this—cook, camp, play in the water, eat pizza. I mean, I haven't done any of those things in a very long time."

"Since your wife died."

He stopped, his expression hardening. "No, not in a long time."

"So this is new for you?"

"New, but a reminder of things I've missed over the years."

Shanna understood how hard this was for him. "And it hurts to remember?"

"Yes." The one word was drawn out in a slow breath, as if it also hurt to speak it. "I need you to understand—it's you. It's because of you."

She wanted to understand. She wanted him to say the words that he couldn't say. Nodding, Shanna stepped back to stare up at him. "Where are we going with this, Simon?"

"I don't know. That part scares me. And that's what I'm trying to say. I like you but this all happened so fast. I might want to… see you again after this week if over."

Her heart hadn't anticipated that sweet,

strained admission. "Okay. I'd like that. No pressure, no rush."

"Yeah?"

"Yes."

He dropped her arms and turned around to stir the chili. "Could you hand me the garlic powder?"

Shanna found the spice and gave it to him, her smile soft and sure. "Here you go."

Simon looked up, briefly, to return that smile. "Thank you."

And that caused her heart to open, truly open. Her whole system tingled and fluttered to life—just from that quick, confident smile.

Was this how it felt, falling in love? All itchy and tingly and electric? Or did she just have a case of poison ivy?

Chapter Fifteen

Simon woke, startled by Shiloh's fierce barking.

"It's just a storm," he said, pushing the dog away. But Shiloh wouldn't shut up. "What is it, boy?"

Then Simon heard it. A banging. Somebody was knocking at the back door. Dressing quickly, he moved down the stairs and flipped on lights.

Brady stood outside, wet and wearing his pajamas.

The boy looked scared to death.

"What is it?" Simon asked after opening the door. The wind pushed at Brady's back, sending wet sheets of rain inside the cabin. Simon pulled the kid inside and shut the door.

"It's Miss Shanna. She doesn't like storms, I guess. Something's wrong with her. She won't let us into her room. She says she's okay, but—"

Simon pulled two raincoats off the hall tree. "Let's go."

Shiloh ran out ahead of them, barking and scratching at the rental cabin's door. Did the dog know something they didn't?

Simon tried to calm his racing heart, tried to imagine what was going on. Shanna was solid, down-to-earth and dedicated to these kids. She couldn't be having a meltdown.

The thunder and lightning had increased now. The rain was so thick Simon could barely see ahead of him. And the cabin was in total darkness. He glanced toward his house and saw it had gone dark, too. The electricity had gone out.

Brady opened the back door and tugged off his slicker. "This way."

Simon dropped his own coat and hurried up the long hallway to find Pammie and Lavi standing outside Shanna's bedroom door.

"Where's Katie?"

"She wanted to sleep in our room tonight,"

Pammie said. "She's still asleep in one of the bunks."

"What happened?" Simon asked, staring at the closed door, his lungs slamming against his ribs.

"We heard her screaming." Lavi held a hand to her mouth. "She said she had a bad dream. But the electricity went out and she won't let us in."

"She'll let me in," Simon said, thinking he'd break the door down. But he had to stay calm for the girls' sake. "Go back to your rooms and wait. Use your flashlights—no candles. I'll let you know how things are, I promise." He looked over at Brady. "You're in charge. I expect you to keep watch, okay? Make sure everyone is safe and accounted for then stay in your room until I figure this out."

Brady nodded. "Sure."

Simon waited until the hallway was clear, then knocked with two knuckles, so many scenarios playing in his head his brain hurt. "Shanna, it's Simon. Can I come in?"

He heard a rustling followed by a cough. "Just a minute."

Her voice sounded foreign and far away.

The wait was intolerable, each heartbeat seeming like an hour. “Shanna?”

The door creaked open. “Where are the kids?”

“In their rooms, safe. Brady’s taking charge.”

“Go tell them I’m okay, please.”

“I think—”

“Simon, please.”

He let out a rush of breath. “I’m coming right back.”

Brady met him in the hallway.

“Pass the word. She’s okay. I’m going to talk to her.”

Brady looked doubtful in the faint glow of his flashlight. “Yes, sir.”

Simon charged back up the hallway. Shanna’s door was ajar, but he knocked. “Shanna, they’re all fine. Can I come in now?”

“I’ll come out there.”

She opened the door, her flashlight caught in her hands like a light saber. She had on a lightweight cotton robe over her T-shirt and cotton pajamas. Her eyes were red-rimmed. He could see that even in the yellow glow from the flashlight.

"Let me find some candles," he said. "I told the kids not to light any but I think we need a couple in here."

She nodded, glanced around. "Katie—"

"She's asleep in the girls' room."

Shanna sank down on the couch. "I'm sorry I caused such a stir."

He found the long-handled lighter over the fireplace and lit the big candle his mother had bought for the coffee table. "Would you like a fire?"

"No, I'm fine."

"Something to drink?"

"No, Simon. Nothing."

He sat down, his damp clothes sticking to his skin. "Talk to me, Shanna."

She turned to him then, her eyes glistening in the muted darkness. The storm had passed but the rain continued to drip against the eaves of the cabin. He watched as she glanced out into the darkness.

"I—I've never been good in storms."

"The kids said you had a bad dream."

She pushed at her dark hair. "Yes, a doozy. I haven't had that dream in a very long time."

He leaned closer. "Why don't you tell me about it?"

A stiff laugh escaped her lips. "I wanted to tell you last night but the boys got into that fight and…I decided I didn't want to tell you after all. I guess the stress of this week finally caught up with me."

"Shanna, listen to me. If you need to talk—"

"I do. I do. It's just usually when I have the dream and then I tell someone *why* I have the dream, usually it freaks people out and they…go away."

"I won't do that."

She looked at him, her eyes big and bright with doubt. "I want us to be friends, Simon."

"I want that, too. But you're scaring me. What's so bad you can't talk about it with me?"

"I told you—after my mother and step-father died," she said, the words rushing out, "I went to live with my aunt and uncle. It happened back in Texas. We moved to Savannah after it happened."

He sat back, turning closer to her. "Yes, I remember. You said you had a bad childhood." All this time, he'd felt so very sorry for himself. He'd wanted isolation so he could grieve, when she'd obviously tried to surround herself with people so she wouldn't grieve. "How did they die?"

She stood up then, her pacing nervous with energy. She looked down the hall then back at him, her words for his ears only. "My father left when I was a baby. Then when I was around ten, my mother remarried. My stepfather abused my mother but she wouldn't leave him. When he started hitting me, she still wouldn't leave him. But she was willing to leave me behind to go with him. So my aunt and uncle came and got me and for a couple of years things were better for me, but when I was almost thirteen, my mother came home and managed to get me back. I don't know the details about how she did it, or why she even bothered to take me back. She was still with him."

Simon got up and reached for her, but she turned away. "Let me finish, okay?"

He couldn't speak. He couldn't believe this incredible woman, the woman with the quick smile and the joy of Christ in her heart, was standing here telling him this horrible, unbelievable story. He couldn't believe that a grown man would hit her, beat her. He thought of little Katie and now understood so much more why Shanna loved and protected the little girl. She'd been through the same thing.

"I was back with them about a week when it happened again. He got drunk and beat my mother and because I was crying, he came after me. My mother tried to pull him off of me. He hit her one last time. She fell and she never got up. She just never got up."

"Shanna..."

"It's okay. I'm okay. It's—when storms come, I remember. It was storming that night, a terrible storm. She and I were scared. But he laughed at us. Laughed at us, Simon. Then he got mad and started lashing out, the way he always did. It was because—inside—he was so afraid of life, so afraid of giving up the bottle. He was the one who was really scared."

She went to stare out the big window, the darkness surrounding her. Simon walked over to stand by her, not daring to touch her. But he so wanted to hold her and tell her it was all right now. He was here and he'd keep her safe. But would she believe him?

"He left after he hit her. Just left me there with her. I cried and tried to wake her up, but she wouldn't move. I called my aunt and she came." She gulped, a sob escaping. "They didn't tell me anything. The ambulance came and they took her to the hospital. I went with my aunt and uncle. The next day, they told me my mother had died from a brain injury." She let out another little sob. "And two days later, my stepfather was so upset, he was driving his car drunk and he had a wreck and ran into a tree. He was killed on impact."

She put her hand against the windowsill. "I dreamed about the storm and that night. He was hitting me with a big belt. I saw him hit my mother and watched her fall to the floor. I woke up screaming." She leaned against the window. "I didn't want to upset the children. I'm so sorry."

He touched her then, pulling her toward him. "Shanna, Shanna."

She finally came into his arms. “Don’t. I can’t take your pity. I can’t.”

Simon wanted to scream his rage. The very thing he’d feared—the pity of others—the thing that had kept him so secluded and shuttered—was also the thing that had forced her to live life to the fullest, to be the happy, nurturing person she’d become. Grief had driven both of them to this spot. God had brought them together.

“I don’t pity you, Shanna. I admire you and respect you. I can’t believe you’ve held this in for so long.”

She pulled away, wiped her eyes. “I went through a lot of therapy but I rebelled big time against all that therapy. I acted out a lot as a teenager.” She seemed to straighten, some of the brightness back. “Then I got involved in church and I found out it wasn’t my fault. My aunt kept telling me that, but I didn’t believe her. You see, I never thought Christ could love someone like me. My own father left me, my stepfather seemed to hate me and my mother didn’t fight for me, no matter how good I tried to be. Why should God love me?”

“He does,” Simon told her, his fingers

tracing her tears. "He does. How could the Lord not love you?"

She stared up into Simon's eyes, her expression bordering on surprise. "This is the part where most men run in the other direction. I've tried this both ways—not talking about it or pouring my heart out and telling the whole ugly story. Neither way works. You don't have to stay, Simon. I'm used to dealing with this on my own."

"I'm not leaving," he said, pulling her back into his arms, all of his protective instincts crying out inside that rage that seemed to fill his soul. "I'm not leaving you, Shanna."

She hesitated, held back, then looked up at him and fell into his arms. "I'm such a bother."

A bother.

Simon held her there on the couch, thinking she *was* a bother. A beautiful, bright, sparkling, life-changing bother.

He liked being bothered by her.

And he thanked God she had somehow survived and overcome her terrible childhood because that had brought her to these children, and that had brought her to him. When he compared his growing up with what she must have been through, Simon knew he'd been one of the blessed ones. He'd had a loving set of parents who believed in discipline, not abuse. He had a brother who was willing to fight for him, even when Simon pushed him away. He'd had Marcy as a true blessing and now, God had somehow found a way to show Simon that he could live again. God had sent him Shanna. Some bother.

For a while, he sat there holding her, his fingers brushing through her long, silky hair. He let her cry, let her hold on to him, let her see that he wasn't going to leave until she was better, much better. And he probably wouldn't leave even then. He'd be here, right here, next door and hopefully, in her life, from now on.

"How ya doing?" he asked on a soft whisper in her ear.

"Better." She glanced up at him. "You're so warm."

"Are you cold?"

"Not anymore."

She settled back against him, her body

finally relaxing into a light gentle sleep. Simon didn't dare move, so he closed his eyes and cuddled her close while he watched the candle's lifting flame weaving and dancing in the dark night.

A few minutes later, he heard a noise in the hallway and looked up to find a group huddled there. The kids.

"Is she all right?" Brady asked, creeping forward.

"She's fine," Simon said, praying it was so. And praying they hadn't heard anything. "How long y'all been there?"

Brady stepped a little closer. "We only came out when things got too quiet. We didn't want to bother you."

Simon almost laughed out loud at that one.

"Nobody's bothering me, son. But I appreciate you giving Miss Shanna some much needed space."

Shanna sat up then, her eyes bleary. "Did I fall asleep?"

"Yeah. We have visitors."

She looked over the couch. "Oh, my. C'mon in. It's okay. Where's Katie?"

"Still sleeping away," Pammie said, rushing to sit on the coffee table. "Miss Shanna, that must have been a horrible dream."

Shanna looked over at Simon, her smile soft. "It was, Pammie. But...it's over now."

"Can we make hot chocolate?" Lavi asked.

"And popcorn?" Robert suggested. "The electricity is back on."

"I think that's a great idea." Simon gave Shanna a soft touch on her arm. "Sit. I'll take care of it."

She shot him a grateful look. "Okay."

He went to the kitchen then turned to find Pammie hugging Shanna's neck. Then one by one, the other kids did the same. He had to turn around and swallow the lump in his throat while he searched for the hot-chocolate mix.

Chapter Sixteen

The rain came down all night long.

Simon and Shanna sat with the kids by a nice, roaring fire, and played board games and charades while the electricity flickered on and off.

"It's late," Simon finally told the kids. "Go on to bed. You can probably sleep late since the weather radio says this rain will be with us all day and well into the weekend."

"Tomorrow's our last day," Lavi said, her mouth turning into a pretty pout. "We were going to have a talent show out on the deck."

"Too wet for that now, honey," Shanna said, stifling a yawn. She didn't think she could face Simon in the light of morning.

Not yet. So she did what she'd always done when she couldn't face something. She focused on the here and now. "We might do a shorter version of our talent show in here. Or we might just head back into town early."

They all groaned on that one.

"It'll be nice to sleep in," Brady said with a grin. Then he gave Shanna a hard stare. "Are you sure you're better now?"

Shanna glanced toward Simon. Why had she had the dream, now of all times and places? "I'm fine, really. It was a horrible dream. The thunder scared me. I didn't like storms when I was little. I guess I still don't."

"You never told us that," Pammie said, her gaze questioning. "You don't talk much about when you were a little girl."

"No, I don't," Shanna replied, sorry that she's scared the kids. "Some things are hard to talk about."

Pammie seemed to accept that answer. "You always let us talk about anything."

And for good reason, Shanna wanted to say. "Yes, I do. I want you to be able to come to me if you need me, no matter what."

Katie came pattering into the room, wiping at her eyes. "What's going on?"

All the older kids laughed.

"You slept through the storm," Felix said, his skin covered with pink-colored calamine lotion.

"What storm?" Katie went straight to Simon and climbed up in his lap. "What are you doing here?"

Shanna smiled at that. Katie trusted the man. Shiloh, asleep by the fire, trusted the man. The kids had trusted him to come to her rescue last night.

And she'd trusted him with her deepest fears and her worst secret. Maybe now, he could trust her a little bit, too.

She looked around and saw the youthful faces of these children she'd come to love. This week had changed them. She could see it in their eyes when they listened to her devotionals and when they asked questions about the Bible and Christ. She could see it in the way Brady's attitude toward Pammie had changed from demanding and overbearing to caring and respectful. She could see it in how Felix and Marshall, once at each other's throats, now laughed and talked and made plans together. She could see it in the way Robert and Lavi played checkers together and helped serve the hot chocolate. And she could certainly see the difference in Katie's trusting attitude. The little girl was healing.

And so was Shanna.

Finally, she told the kids to go to bed. "Snuggle in. We'll stay inside until the rain lets up. Then we'll check the weather and make a decision about going back to town early. No point in staying here if it's going to keep raining. Sometimes, when it rains like this, the road back to town can get washed out. Or so I've been told by the locals."

One by one, they marched off to their rooms, the girls taking Katie with them again.

The quietness settled over Shanna and Simon like a warm blanket, the crackle of the fire's last embers comforting and cozy.

"Long night," he said, waiting for her to sit down. "C'mon and rest. I'll clean up."

Shanna was suddenly tired and sleepy. "Okay. But I'm sure you're exhausted."

"Actually, I'm fine." He gave her a measuring, all-encompassing look that left her feeling open and vulnerable. "And I think it's my turn to talk."

Shanna was wide awake after that comment. "I'm listening."

He tugged her close, kissed the top of her head. "I loved Marcy so much."

"I know." Her heart tripped over itself. Was he ready for this? Was she?

"I didn't think I'd ever get over losing her. I couldn't face people. The kind words, the patronizing comments, the platitudes that didn't help. So I decided to give up and stay here, safe in the woods. I had my work."

She looked up at him, saw the fear in his face. "Understandable. It's hard to lose somebody you love."

"And you know that, too. So much more than I ever have. Does Cari know about what happened to you?"

"Yes, but we don't talk about it. I made her promise not to tell anyone."

"You held your grief inside while I showed mine to anyone who dared to confront me."

"We're a pair of oddballs, aren't we?"

He lifted her chin, his dark gaze capturing her in a sweet longing. “Yes, we certainly are.” He kissed her then, a gentle feather of a touch on her lips. “There’s so much more I need to say—”

She stopped his words with her own kiss, to show him that sometimes words weren’t necessary to convey feelings.

Simon accepted that and pulled her close, his lips moving over hers with relief and finally, acceptance. She felt that acceptance in the way he sighed and gave in, at last, to his feelings for her.

Later, as the dark skies lightened to a dreary dawn, she waved to him and then watched him walk back through the soggy wildflowers to his cabin, Shiloh trotting ahead to wait on the porch for his reluctant master.

Shanna stood at her spot on the deck, making sure they got inside. Then she turned to get on with her day.

And realized she’d fallen in love with the bootmaker.

He’d fallen in love with the youth counselor.

Simon stood in the middle of his workshop, the smell of leather covering him like an old jacket. Maybe if he poured himself back into his work, he could figure out how to handle loving Shanna. After making a pot of coffee, he cranked up the radio and waited for the familiar twang of country songs to fuel his angst. But a weather report interrupted the next set of songs.

"This latest round of thunderstorms promises to be even stronger than the ones that passed through last night. Expect more rain, possibly several inches. Watch for flash flooding on the roads and near the river. Let's be cautious out there, folks. If you don't have to be out in this, stay inside. More details on our next report."

Simon usually didn't give such reports much thought, but with Shanna and the kids next door, he couldn't deny the sense of dread filling his heart. He went to the back porch and stared down at the Chattahoochee. The river had risen several feet over night.

And Simon knew what that meant. It could flood its banks. They'd all be trapped in that cabin perched up on the hillside.

The family cabin was pretty secure since they'd built it up on a high bluff. But the two smaller cabins were down closer to the river.

It had been a long time, maybe twenty years, since they'd had a major flood along the river. But it could happen again. Certainly, with the promise of more heavy rains, it could happen before nightfall.

He had to get Shanna and those kids out of here before the water got any higher.

They'd had a late breakfast and were now laughing at the antics of Felix and Marshall's duet of "If I Had A Hammer" when Shanna heard a knock on the back door.

"It's Mr. Simon," Katie said, rushing to the door.

Shanna smiled as he entered, but after seeing the concerned look in his eyes she got up and hurried to meet him. "Hi."

He looked around. "I hate to interrupt but the weather is getting worse. They're predicting more storms and heavy rains. That means flash flooding on the roads and possible flooding on the river. This cabin is on a low spot. It could get messy."

"Do we need to leave early?" she asked, worry sending a quiver of concern down her spine.

"I think so. Like now. It's already rained another two inches since dawn. I know you had someone else help bring some of the kids out, so I can take some of them in my delivery van if you can get a few in your SUV."

"That would work. What about your workshop and cabin?"

"Workshop is a ways back from the river. Our big cabin should be okay. But this one and my mom's smaller one might be in trouble. After I drop y'all off, I'll get Rick and some of the guys to help me sandbag the banks just in case."

Telling herself Simon was capable of handling this, Shanna tamped down her fears. "I'll explain to the children."

She turned to where Felix and Marshall were finishing up then waited for the kids to give them a round of applause.

"Listen up, people," she said, clapping

her hands together. "The weather is getting worse. This rain might cause some flooding between here and town and the river could get really high and flood our cabin. We need to leave before the roads become impassable. So I need you to pack up your stuff and clean up your rooms. The sooner we can get back to town and higher ground, the better."

"Ah, man. I wanted to do my solo," Robert replied.

"I know," Shanna said. "We'll have the talent show back at church, maybe on Sunday night, okay?"

Mumbles and groans followed but they all got up and started gathering games and blankets.

"Don't worry about cleaning up too much," Simon said to her. "We'll take care of that later."

Shanna went about the business of gathering supplies, her gaze scanning the downpour outside. She had to get the kids to safety. That thought kept her from going into full panic mode.

* * *

An hour later, wet from sloshing back and forth through the unrelenting rain, they were loaded up and ready to go.

Simon came around the big van, his black rain coat dripping water. "Okay, I'll lead and you stay right behind me. I'll go slow so I can keep you in my sight."

"We'll be fine," Shanna told him, glancing back at Katie and Robert. Brady rode shotgun with her while Pammie, Lavi, Felix and Marshall rode with Simon and Shiloh in the van. "Everyone's buckled in and Brady's going to help me watch for washouts."

"Good." He leaned in, his eyes rich with unspoken hope. "Be careful."

Shanna swallowed back the swirling awareness cresting inside her heart. "We will. I promise."

He stepped back, his gaze holding hers for a brief moment. Then he turned and hurried to get into the van.

Shanna cranked up, wondering if she'd see him again soon. Wondering if she'd just dreamed the new closeness between them.

Please, Lord, open Simon's heart to love again, she prayed. Then she took one last glance at the quaint little cabin where she'd fallen in love with Simon Adams.

Chapter Seventeen

Simon thought about her pretty smile. Even with soaking wet hair and no makeup, Shanna had a smile that didn't diminish one bit in gloomy weather.

He loved that about her.

He loved everything about her.

These foreign, exciting, scary thoughts rolled through his head with each rumble of thunder as they slowly made their way down the winding mountain road toward Knotwood.

He'd think about all of that once he knew Shanna and the kids were safe. Hitting his cell phone, he called ahead to Rick. "We're on our way. Have you lined up sandbags?"

Rick grunted over the line. "Me and

everyone else who owns a place out on the river. We've already sandbagged most of the banks here in town. Hopefully, all the buildings are high enough up to prevent any major flooding. But I have to tell you, brother, I'm worried. The water's lapping at the high bank right behind the Pizza Haus. Another foot or two and it'll run over the back deck."

Simon checked in his rearview mirror and saw Shanna's car making the curve behind him. "Yeah, same on the lower banks out at the cabins. I'm worried about the rental cabin the most. It's on that low ledge right near where the river curves. Thought it best to move everybody into town."

"Good idea. Hopefully, we can get out there before nightfall and get something going," Rick replied. "Gotta go. It's crazy here. Drive safe."

Simon hung up then shot Pammie a reassuring smile. "We'll be there soon."

Lavi looked at him from the back seat. "I'm glad you're here, Mr. Simon."

"Me, too, Lavi. Me, too."

He took another glance in the rearview, watching as Shanna's car came over the hill behind them. As long as everyone was safe, he could handle anything else.

Shanna kept her gaze focused on the sleek, winding road, the taillights of Simon's van working like a beacon to carry her home. She had so much she wanted to say to him, so much she wanted to ask him. This feeling, so completely exhilarating and refreshing, left her breathless with possibilities and reveling in a newfound hope. She couldn't wait to call Aunt Claire and tell her that at long last, she had found a man who had staying power.

Katie sneezed. "My nose itches."

Shanna looked in the mirror, seeing the little girl's sweet reflection. "I hope you're not coming down with a cold."

"I want my grandma," Katie said, her request brave and quiet.

"Almost there, honey. Another few miles."

Shanna glanced back at the road. Where had Simon gone? She steered the car around a winding curve, relieved to see the van off in the distance. Then she hit a pothole and the whole car shook. "Wow, that was a deep one."

"Here comes another one," Brady said, pointing toward the water running across the road.

The SUV dipped, hitting hard against another washed-out hole where asphalt had once been. Shanna braced, hitting the brakes so she could guide the vehicle out of the hole. She pushed on the gas, shoving the vehicle up and out then accelerated again.

And that's when a young doe came bounding across the road. Shanna screamed, slamming on brakes and turning the wheel to avoid the deer. The SUV skidded on the wet road and swerved into a crooked spin. Then it went careening toward a big pine leaning across a washed out ravine.

Simon heard the crash before he saw it.

Then with a sick feeling twisting the pit of his stomach, he slammed on brakes and looked in the mirror. Shanna's car bolted off the road and into a shallow ravine filled with muddy water.

Simon took a heaving breath, his pulse pounding so hard against his temple, he thought he might pass out. "Pammie, call 911! Shanna's had a wreck."

The girl took his phone then turned to look back behind them. "Are they gonna be all right?"

"I hope so, honey. Just call, right now. And stay inside the van."

He ran through the driving rain, prayers slipping and sliding in his mind while his boots sloshed through the water running over the road.

Please, God. Please, God. Please, God, his pulse beat over and over. *Please.*

When he got to the car, Brady was sitting up, a gash bleeding on his forehead. "What happened?" Simon called out as he reached the passenger side.

Brady looked shocked and scared. "A deer. We...she swerved and lost control."

Simon looked over to where Shanna lay still and silent, her head against the steering wheel. Why hadn't the air bag deployed? Maybe because she hadn't been going that fast. But fast enough to hit a tree. The spin had sent her right toward the tree, the jolt off the road hitting hard.

Then he heard crying. "Katie? Talk to me, baby. Are you all right?"

"Scared. I want outta here."

Robert lifted up. "I think I'm okay. My head hit the roof." He put a hand on Katie's arm. "I tried to shield Katie."

"Good, that's good," Simon said. "Sit tight. I know you're scared, but don't move. We've called for help."

"What about Miss Shanna?" Brady asked, pushing at her arm. "She's not waking up, Simon. Do something!"

Simon rushed around the car, his legs sinking in the knee-deep water. The driver-side door and windshield had rammed at an angle against the trunk of the pine tree. "I don't know if I can get to her."

But he had to get to her. Stomping through the mud and bramble, he pressed his body against the SUV. "Shanna? Shanna, can you hear me?"

She didn't move. Her dark hair fell around her face, her eyes were closed, and blood was running down her temple.

Simon had never felt so helpless in his life. "Brady, come here."

The boy hurried around the SUV. Katie started crying again and Robert stared out through the shattered glass of Shanna's window, his expression fixated on Simon.

Simon grabbed Brady by the arm. "We're going to try and pry the door open as far as we can get it, okay?"

Brady nodded, his skin pale. "It's just like what happened to me. I survived." He looked over at Simon, tears in his eyes, rain soaking his blond hair. "I survived, Simon."

Simon prayed the same would happen this time. He couldn't lose Shanna, not now. Not like this.

He'd never had the chance to tell her how much he loved her.

Simon paced the hospital corridor, the throng of people around him blurring into the background as he relived the horror of Shanna's wreck. He should have taken them all to the big cabin. They probably would have been safe there, what was he thinking, letting her drive through that washed-out road? He thought about the doe. Shanna had tried not to hit the animal. But he still felt responsible.

They'd tried to get her out, but the door was wedged too tightly against the tree—smashed in a twisted, grotesque way that still made him sick to his stomach. The first responders had to cut the door open to extract her. They couldn't bring her over the passenger seat—too dangerous. Severe head trauma. That's what they'd called it. She didn't wake up, even when they'd put a heavy neck brace on her. After the neurologist had been called in, they'd taken her away to surgery.

Brady had a contusion, but stitches had fixed that. Katie and Robert were all right, thank goodness. Just some scratches and bruises. Katie's grandparents had come to take her home. The little girl was frightened and crying when they left.

Simon knew the feeling. He wanted to cry. He couldn't cry. His fears were wedged somewhere between his heart and his stomach, the sight of Shanna's still, pale face as they'd carried her away on a stretcher scaring him beyond reason. Scaring him and making him relive memories he'd tried to bury. He hated this hospital. He hated this familiar, sickening feeling. He wanted so badly to leave, but he'd told Shanna he wouldn't leave her. Could he live up to that vow?

Brady walked over to him. "Why haven't we heard anything?" The kid's eyes were bloodshot, his expression fierce with worry.

Simon wondered that same thing. He glanced over at Brady. "I don't know. How's your head?"

"I'm fine," Brady said. "Miss Shanna took the brunt of the crash."

"Seems she's been doing that most of her life."

Brady looked confused then shrugged. "Everyone's praying. Even my mom is here. She actually likes Shanna."

"Who doesn't?" Simon said, his head pounding.

Rick and Cari surrounded him. "Mom's doing her thing with the prayer chain," Rick said. "She's on the phone right now."

Simon had to wonder if that would work. They'd all prayed for Marcy and God had called her home. His mother told him their prayers had been answered. Marcy was no longer in pain, no longer sick. She was healed.

That kind of healing in heaven sure didn't help those left here on earth.

"I don't think I can go through this again," he said to Rick under his breath. "I don't think—"

Rick held his shoulder, his fingers digging in. "Simon, hold on. Just hold on. I'm here. Mom's here. We're all here. Shanna's aunt and uncle are on their way from Savannah."

Simon turned to his brother, despair pulling at him. "Rick, help me. I don't know if—"

The doors from ICU burst open and the doctor who'd operated on Shanna came striding toward them. Simon inhaled a shuddered breath, his prayers frozen and abstract. He wished he were back in his studio, clueless and miserable. He could handle being alone. He couldn't handle losing Shanna so soon after falling for her.

Dr. Mercer folded his hands together. "Is her next of kin here yet?"

"About an hour out," Rick said. "This weather has made it slow going. Can you tell us anything, doctor? Please?"

The tall doctor nodded. "She's had a traumatic brain injury. But the surgery went as well as expected. We've relieved the pressure on her brain and now all we can do is wait. Since I already went over the complications with all of you earlier, you know the risk involved."

"Wait? What does that mean?" Simon said, stepping forward. "Is she going to wake up?"

The doctor gave them a sympathetic look. "She's in a coma. We don't know when she'll come out of it and when and if she does wake up, she might have complications. I'm sorry. We have to be patient now. Her body is trying to heal and we have to let her rest. But we'll continue to do tests on her to identify her responsiveness to stimuli. If all goes well, she'll wake up and be fine. She might require some rehabilitation or she might not ever fully recover."

"And if things don't go well?" Cari asked, tears falling down her face. "What should we expect?"

"It's hard to say. She might have some amnesia, short-term or long-term, and her rehabilitation might take longer. In other words, she might have to relearn some things. Worst case scenario, she might not ever be the same. But we have state-of-the-art drugs and we've had wonderful results with the latest rehabilitation techniques."

Simon couldn't settle for that. He had to fight for her, make her well again. "I need to see her."

"She's in recovery right now. No visitors yet. And then only family."

"We *are* family," he said, his fists curled at his side. "We're her family. She shouldn't be alone."

"I'll see what I can do," the doctor told him. "I'll let you know when you can visit her."

Simon turned around and saw all the people gathered here, people who loved Shanna and believed she would be all right. Brady stood with his mother, Doreen, his expression full of sorrow. The kid refused to leave. The others had been hustled away by their parents, but Simon knew they'd be back. They wouldn't abandon Shanna.

He wouldn't abandon her either. He'd promised her he'd stay. And now, somehow, no matter how much it destroyed him to be back in this place, he'd live up to that promise.

He looked up to find his mother staring at him. "Simon, you need to rest."

"I can't rest, Ma," he said, walking toward her.

Gayle took him into her arms, hugging him close. "I'm here, son. I'm here."

Simon looked up at his mother, saw the love and concern in her eyes. "I fell in love again. I did. I tried not to, but I love her. It happened so fast—this thing with us. Now this—why did this have to happen? Why didn't I keep them out on the river until the weather got better?"

"You did the right thing," Gayle said, patting his shoulders. "It could be much worse out there. It's been raining non-stop all night. You had no way of knowing, Simon. It's not your fault."

But he shouldered the blame. And he wished with all his heart he didn't have to go through this again. Not with Shanna. Not so soon after he'd come alive again, because of her.

He held onto his mother's hands, fighting tears that couldn't be released. He needed help. Real help. "Ma, where's the hospital chapel?"

Gayle couldn't stop her tears. "I'll show you. I'll go with you."

She took him by the hand and together, they walked down the long hallway to find a place where Simon could be alone with his prayers. And back in the Lord's loving arms.

Chapter Eighteen

He prayed for what seemed like hours. He stayed and prayed long after his mother had gone back to check on Shanna and work on the prayer chain.

Simon poured out all his angst to God, starting with Marcy's illness and death, his bitterness and how he'd decided to hide out from the world and on to meeting Shanna and the youth group.

He hadn't come into the chapel when Marcy was sick. He didn't want to talk to God back then. He was angry at God and everyone else who still walked and lived and breathed. He didn't think his heart would ever recover. He held that heart away, inside a cocoon of grief and anger, like a shield of armor. Shanna had pulled through that armor, her sword a soft whisper of unyielding faith.

But now, things were different. Simon knew in order to survive this ordeal, he needed a power stronger than himself. He needed the Lord.

"You wouldn't bring me here to destroy me yet again, would you, Lord? Please help me to understand? Please, Lord?"

He told God about Shanna, about how she'd made a difference in so many lives, but especially the lives of the seven children she'd taken under her wing.

"She wanted to help them and protect them, Lord. Don't take her now. Don't change her life. She's a teacher. She needs to be alive and laughing and teaching and loving."

He leaned into the pew in front of him, his head down on his arms, his fingers wrapped together. "I need her, Lord. I love her. It took me so long to...love again."

Simon waited, the silence of the still peaceful sanctuary wrapping him in a shimmering quiet. He remained still and listening, but inside his heart was shouting for release, for a sign, for hope. Any hope.

Then he heard the door creaking open and lifted his head to find an older woman coming down the aisle toward him. She was plump and petite, with reddish brown hair and a warm smile.

"Simon?"

He stood, his bones and joints stiff from sitting for so long. "Yes, ma'am."

The woman reached out her hand. "I'm Claire Murphy. Shanna's aunt."

Simon shook her hand, barely able to speak. "You made it."

"Yes, we got here a little while ago." She patted his hand. "I wanted to thank you, for helping Shanna. For being there with her."

"I didn't do much."

"I think you did," Claire said, her eyes brimming with tears. "Shanna called me a couple of times this week. We like to stay in touch. She mentioned you quite a bit."

"She did?"

"Yes." She didn't elaborate, but her smile said it all. "Would you like to go in and see her?"

Simon's heart hurt with such a sweet

emotion, he thought he might have to sit back down. "I'd like that, yes, ma'am."

"Come with me then. Her Uncle Doug is with her now, but we'll give you some time with her."

They walked back down the long hallway toward the ICU waiting room. His mother was still there. Cari and Brady were sitting in a corner, talking quietly. People were milling about. Jolena was setting up snacks near the coffee bar. Doreen Duncan paced the floor, a phone to her ear, her gaze hitting on her son every few seconds.

Everyone loved Shanna.

Claire led him past the group hovering in the waiting room. When they entered the big double doors to the ICU, Simon braced himself. He wouldn't give in to his fears or his tears. He just wanted to see Shanna.

Claire lead him into a big room with all sorts of beeping machines and IVs, all hooked up to the small figure lying so still and pale in the bed.

Simon nodded to the gray-haired man holding Shanna's hand then stood at the end of the bed. Her head was bandaged all the way around. He thought about her beautiful long dark hair, a tear forming in his right eye.

Hair could grow back.

The man moved away. "Hi, I'm Doug." Then he motioned for Simon to step forward. Simon shook his hand, hoping the man didn't feel the trembling in Simon's fingers. Another tear formed in his left eye. He blinked, tried to focus.

Shanna's aunt and uncle left the room. Simon watched them walk away, his mind screaming for them to stay and hold him up. But he could do this. He could do this for Shanna. Blocking out the ragged, torn memories of Marcy's death, he held Shanna's bed and willed her to wake up.

He made it to the side of the stark, sterile bed, another tear slipping down his face. Then he took her hand in his. Her hands were so tiny. He knew that, but he'd never actually thought about how fragile, how delicate she truly was. Simon held her with a gentle touch, afraid he'd break her if he held too tight. More tears. He hated tears.

"Shanna?" He cleared his throat, swallowed. "Shanna, it's me, Simon. You need to wake up, sweetheart. C'mon, and wake up and talk to me, bother me, please? Shanna, please. We need you. We all need you. I need you."

He sat down in the chair by the bed, both of his hands gripping hers now. "Shanna, you're gonna be all right. The doctor says you'll wake up. You're just tired and hurt. You need to rest and get better. But we want you to come back to us. We want you to wake up and see all the people who love you."

He cried now, accepting the tears that he'd held in for so many years. Tears of frustration and pain, of longing and remorse, tears of regret and redemption.

"Shanna, we love you." And finally, "I love you. Just give me a chance to tell you that, please."

She didn't move. Didn't respond. So Simon sat and watched her, talking to her as the day turned into night. The light behind the drawn blinds turned to shadows, the noises of the hospital drowned out by the settling of the day and the steady cadence of the rain outside.

Nurses came and went, checking her.

The doctors did test after test while Simon waited impatiently outside.

He insisted on staying with her, no matter the rules, no matter the pitiful stares. "I promised her I wouldn't leave her," he explained to the hospital staff. "I can't leave her. She shouldn't be alone."

And so he was allowed to stay. He lost track of the time. He prayed. He dozed. He held her hand. He didn't eat. He barely slept. He talked to her, reminding her of the hotdogs and the fire he'd put out, reminding her of how much fun they'd had riding the river. He relived showing Shanna and the kids his studio, telling her how much he enjoyed doing that.

"I'm making you a pretty pair of boots," he said. "Light brown with hearts of gold and wildflowers."

The hours merged together. Fatigue pulled at him, but he stayed. When they forced him out for another round of tests and picking and probing, he drank massive amounts of coffee and shoved bits and pieces of food down his throat until he was allowed back in.

Until finally late one night, his brother

grabbed him by the arm and pulled him to the side. "You need a shower."

Simon blinked, saw the concern on Rick's face. "I don't want to leave."

"Okay, we all get that you love her. You've shown that, Simon. She knows it. But you've been here for three days now and if she wakes up and finds you looking like you just came out of hibernation, you're going to scare her and confuse her."

"She'll be confused. The doctors keep telling me that. I've been here for three days?"

Rick nodded. "The river's already receded and we're all fine, high and dry, thankfully. Just go and rest over at the general store apartment or at Duncan House. Get a shower and take a nap. I'll call you if—"

"I can't leave her, Rick. I'm not going."

Rick put his hands on Simon's shoulders. "Mom told me you'd say that. So I brought fresh clothes, some toiletries and the hospital has a bed you can use to rest. Get cleaned up and sleep for one hour. You aren't going to help her if you collapse."

Simon followed his brother, too tired to argue. He'd get a quick shower, then give

Rick the slip and go back to Shanna. "You make somebody watch out for her."

"I will," Rick said. "Go."

He took a shower, the hot water hitting him like a warm rain. He cleaned up, put on the clothes and sat down on the bed. Then he closed his eyes and fell back, just for a minute. He was out the minute he hit the soft pillow.

A siren woke him.

Simon looked at the clock by the bed. Eight o'clock in the morning. Had he slept all night?

He jumped up so fast, his head started spinning. Taking a breath, he held tight to the wall and made it to the door. He had to get back to Shanna.

Rick was waiting with a cup of coffee.

Simon took the coffee and kept on walking.

"Hey?"

"You didn't wake me up."

"You needed to rest. Simon?"

He whirled, glaring at Rick. "What?"

Rick gaze held his. "No change."

Simon threw the rest of the coffee in the

trash then motioned to one of the nurses inside the ICU. She nodded.

But when he got to Shanna's room, he saw that she was in the same spot. Still silent and unmoving. What if she never woke up?

Three hours later, Simon sat rubbing Shanna's arm, whispering to her, wishing she'd open her eyes. Her aunt and uncle had come in to visit. Simon took a break while they sat with Shanna, but now he was back and feeling better. He'd eaten, he was clean and he was rested. He wanted this to be over.

The doctors couldn't predict when she'd wake up.

No one could.

He'd have to make a decision soon. He'd have to face the truth and get back to work.

Work. He'd somehow forgotten work.

One more day, Lord, he thought. *One more day with her and then...I'll leave it in Your hands.* What more could he do? He wouldn't leave her. He'd come every day, for as long as it took. He'd come after work.

Or he'd stop working altogether. Somebody had to be here when she woke up. He had to be that somebody.

But in his heart, Simon knew he was slowly giving up. And he also knew if he walked out of this hospital, he'd never be the same again. He'd never recover from this either.

So he lay his head down, praying while he held her hand, hoping against hope that he'd have one more chance to make things right, to find love, to have a child like Katie to love and spoil. To be able to give Shanna the kind of life she deserved. *Just one more chance, Lord.*

A nurse came in and touched his arm. Simon lifted up, ready to do battle. But she held a finger to her lips then pointed to the big window out into the nurses' station.

Simon turned and found seven children of various heights standing outside, staring at him, most of them crying. Brady held little Katie. She lay her head on Brady's shoulder and gave Simon a small, scared smile. Pammie stood there with Lavi, the girls clutching each other. Felix and Marshall stood apart, staring, their eyes wide, their expressions somber. Robert stood with his arms crossed, his head down, watching.

Simon managed a smile and then the tears started falling. He gently let go of Shanna long enough to go outside and hug each child close.

"Thank you for coming," he said. "I'll go tell her y'all are here."

He wiped his eyes, wiped at Lavi's tears, then turned and hurried back to Shanna. "Shanna, sweetheart, you have some visitors. The kids are here. They're worried about you. Why don't you wake up and show them who's boss?"

She didn't move. Simon looked back at the little group hovering in the hallway, aware that the hospital staff had gone beyond the call of duty to help Shanna.

He had to do something. They were all out there, depending on him. Without thinking, he stood up and leaned down, one finger moving over Shanna's pale, still face. Then he lowered his head and kissed her, softly, surely, and with all the love in his heart. He kissed her, whispering endearments, whispering his love.

"I love you," he said, his lips brushing

hers. "We all love you. Please come back to us."

Then he lifted his head and glanced back toward the window, not daring to hope. But one by one, the group of seven lifted their heads and kept a vigil. Then something changed in their somber expressions, and one by one they started grinning.

Because when he turned back to Shanna, her eyes were open.

Three months later

"How's she doing today?"

The attendant smiled at Simon as he rounded the desk toward the rehabilitation center inside the regional hospital. "She's doing great. If she keeps this up, we'll be sending her home in a couple of weeks."

That was the best news Simon could ever hear. He went straight to Shanna's room, the vivid pink lilies and baby's breath bouquet he'd brought held in front of him with one hand, while he tried to hide the big bag in his other hand, holding it behind him. He hoped she'd like his surprise.

"I see you," Shanna said, laughing.

Her laughter sounded like music, sweet, sweet music.

"Are you gonna come in?"

Simon crossed the room to the chair where she sat by the window, sat the vase of flowers on the table, then leaned down to kiss her. "You better believe it."

"Lilies! They're beautiful." She cried a lot these days, through her smiles. It was an effort to get the words out sometimes. But she was getting better every day.

"Not as beautiful as you, sweetheart. How ya doing?"

Shanna wiped at her eyes. "Better. I can read again. Slowly, but I'm reading. My memory is improving, too. But then, you know that, don't you?"

"I sure do." He'd helped with her therapy for three months now, reading to her, holding up flash cards, telling her things she'd forgotten. Telling her over and over about their week together in the spring. She remembered bits and pieces. She remembered him. She didn't remember the crash or the flooding. With therapy, she should be able to teach again, maybe next year.

"You didn't like me," she told him one day. "I almost set the woods on fire."

"Yes, you made a big fire, too big, to cook hotdogs. And you made s'mores and we went rafting on the river. You swam in the secret water hole. We kissed each other on the cabin deck."

"I remember all of that. You made chili and...we talked all night. It was storming."

She remembered most of it now, the good and the bad.

Everyone had helped, from her aunt and uncle to his mother and Jolena and Cari to half the kids at the high school, especially Brady and Pammie, Felix and Marshall, and Lavi and Robert. Katie came by and read her own favorite children's books to Shanna.

"I can't wait to get back to work."

"First things first, my darling."

She grinned. "Our wedding?"

"Our wedding. We'll be married by Christmas."

"I can't wait." She pointed to the big bag, her eyes shining. "What else did you bring me?"

Her positive attitude remained intact, and the doctors agreed it had helped in her recovery. That and her solid faith.

Simon grinned then pulled a box out of the bag. "Oh, just a little something I whipped up for you. For the wedding."

She giggled, sounding like a little girl. But her eyes held his in an all-woman way.

She'd come such a long way over the summer. She was so childlike and so grown up, his Shanna, all in one beautiful, glowing package. She got a little stronger every day.

He thanked God each and every day for her. Simon had promised Shanna he wouldn't leave her. But he'd also made that promise to God, too.

"Simon, are you going to show me what's in that box?"

"Oh, right." He winked then lifted the lid, letting her see.

"Boots? For me?"

"Boots. For you. Just like I promised."

"I thought I'd dreamed that," she said, her eyes holding his. "I thought I'd dreamed it, but these are the boots in that dream. Golden hearts and wildflowers—on boots." She laughed out loud. "I'm wearing these with my wedding dress."

"You better," he said. "Those are a pair of Simon Adams originals. One-of-a-kind, just like you."

Shanna smiled up at him again. "You know I'm such a bother."

"Yes, you sure are."

He put the boots aside then sank down on his knees in front of her. "Just so you keep on bothering me for a long, long time."

"Okay." She leaned into his arms, her spiky new growth of curls tickling his jawbone. "I can do that."

He lifted up. "Time for our afternoon walk. You up to it?"

"Yep. Can I wear my boots?"

"I don't see why not. We'll take it slow and easy."

He explained to her how to put on a pair of custom-made boots and helped her put on some thin socks. Then he helped her slip into the boots by standing behind her and leaning over to tug on the pull straps.

"They feel wonderful," Shanna said, her arm on his as they strolled toward the door. "Do they look okay with my workout clothes?"

"You look beautiful, sweetheart."

Simon escorted her out the side door and down to the park by the river. And together, they walked along the trail and listened to the birds singing and the water flowing. It was a warm day, the drone of bees buzzing nearby reminding Simon that life never stopped.

Shiloh meet them on the path, barking his delight in seeing Shanna. He'd helped with her recovery, too.

"My dog loves you, too," Simon told her, patting her hand. Both the dog and the woman looked at him in surprise.

"Since when did he become your dog?" Shanna asked, grinning.

"Since the day I met you, I think."

"I'm glad then."

"Wanna get married in church, or down by the river?"

"I think church. It might snow."

He nodded. "We could get snowed in."

She leaned her head against his arm

then whispered, "Let's save that part for the honeymoon."

Simon readily agreed to that. They had a lifetime to hide out in seclusion, after all. But he didn't expect that to happen. The world was waiting for them. When he'd kissed Shanna there in the hospital, they'd both come out of a long sleep.

And now, he could take her as his wife, his eyes wide open to the joys of falling in love all over again, with the woman who had become his hometown sweetheart.

* * * * *

Dear Reader,

In this take on Snow White, I wanted to show how a broken recluse and an outgoing optimistic person could learn to get along. I've always been fascinated by people who seem to leave the world behind and rely only on the bare necessities for life.

In the case of Simon Adams, he thought he was surviving just fine by hiding out near the river with the mountains around him. But he wasn't really living until he met Shanna White and saw how she loved life with such joy. The self-exiled widower didn't want to become involved in life again but Shanna and her merry band of seven children pulled at his heart and brought him out of a deep spiritual sleep.

This can happen to anyone who has suffered a great loss, whether it's the death of a loved one or shutting down a relationship with someone close. And this can happen in our faith, when we turn away from God because we are so confused and hurt.

Shanna might have been the one to suffer a coma, but Simon was the one who couldn't wake up and live his faith. With her help and her unyielding faith, he was able to find a true way of living life to the fullest.

I hope this story brings you the same joy it brought to me. Maybe it will show someone out there that it's time to wake up and live life the way God wants us to live—with joy and love. Until next time, may the angels watch over you, always.

Lenora Worth

QUESTIONS FOR DISCUSSION

1. Why was Simon so reclusive and distant? Do you think grief can do this to a person?

2. Why did his brother Rick allow the dog Shiloh to stay with Simon a lot?

3. Shanna suffered a horrible trauma as a child but she overcame it through her faith. How is that different from the way Simon reacted to the death of his wife?

4. Do you think we all hide behind some sort of façade to cover our pain and grief? How can our faith help us to open up more?

5. Have you ever helped a youth who was troubled and confused? Do you think God leads us to do such things?

6. Simon had the strength of family to see him through. How has your family

helped or hindered your own sorrows or hurts?

7. Did Shanna handle the children in a good way? Do you think she made a difference in the lives of these children?

8. Simon tried to deal with Brady and Pammie in a delicate but firm way. Do you believe he did the right thing in talking to them about boundaries in a budding relationship?

9. Why did Shanna fight so hard to help Simon? And why did he try to turn her away?

10. Did you like the town of Knotwood? Why is it that small towns can be a blessing in times of crisis?

11. Why was Simon's work so important to him? Do you think he was the cobbler who had no shoes, faithwise?

12. Brady Stillman played a big part in this story and in the previous book *Hometown Princess*. Do you think Brady will grow up to be a good man?